TO: Am___ ___im

The fi_____ __ out

Soon, *My Girl* Hope

You can come see my

hard work *Got a*

Girlfriend 2

James Tanner
4-11-17

My Girl

Got a

Girlfriend 2

By
James Tanner

My Girl Got a Girlfriend 2
Copyright © 2013 by James G. Tanner, Jr.

Editor/Typesetter: Carla M. Dean (www.ucanmarkmyword.com)
Cover Design: Oddball Dsgn

Printed in the United States of America

First Edition

ISBN-10-digit: 0979709423
ISBN-13-digit: 978-0-9797094-2-5

Copies can be ordered by sending $15.00 plus $5.00 for shipping and handling to:

Park Bench Entertainment, Inc.
C/O James Tanner
P.O. Box 7223
Silver Spring, MD 20907

Acknowledgements

I want to give all praise to God for blessing me with the intelligence to write this book and for guiding me in the right direction and making all this possible.

I want to thank my mother and father, Barbara Tanner and James Tanner, my brother Micheal Tanner, my children Marja', Drake and Damari, my aunt Kim Oliver- Parker, Alardo Parker, Keisha Parker, Melissa Lockhart and the rest of the Lockhart family, MC Lucky, Moka, Babii, Nonchalant, DJ C Sharpe, Butta and Bodacious Ent., Blade and Blade Ent., Editor Carla M. Dean, Mz. Vicki, OOHZEE, Robert "Shaka" Mercer, Lil' Chris and the Downing family Tommy Lay, David "Lucan" Bailey, Curtis Smith, Carl Hunter, Cousin Nicky, Cousin Crystal, Cousin Peaches, Donald Boone, Fat Boy, Darrell King, Cassandra Riddick aka "Smoochie", Frank Sudds, Yolanda, Tunnie and Veda thanks for the kids, Cousin Mikey, Cousin Ashley, Lushy Lush, Amazin, Angela of 21st, Jetta, Mecca Reccio, Taresa Sledge, Tonya aka Ms Bossy, Ms.Tiesha "Ty" Lawrence, Gail Williams, Kurt at 15 and C, Ronald Blue, Jerome Bradshaw, Shermon Bunch, Lonnie, DJ, Smokey B, Smoke D, Veronica Green, Uncle Steve, Aunt Wanda, Aunt Mary and Donald, Andre, Skip, Tay, Mya Macoy, Viva and Secret Weapon Ent. Vernon and Wilmont Rush, Chantal Mason, Cousin Shantel and Lil' Sam, Cousin Crystal Martin, Ray Allen, William Johnson, Valarie Lewis, Charnika Edwards, Tuffy, French Kiss, Beautiful, Ladonna Mitchell, Ke Ke the

Barber, Beaver, my lawyer Brain McDaniels, Broadway and Chyna Black, my graphic artist Davida Baldwin, Don Scott, Walter Brown, Donald "Donnie" Thomas, Margret and the Skylark crew, Derrick Pumphry, my entertainment attorney Fred Samuels, Joanne Hudson, Karen Gray Houston and Fox 5 News, Sam Ford and Channel 7 News Center, my five thousand Facebook friends, My Girl Got A Girlfriend Facebook fans, my YouTube page friends, the whole LGBT Community, Reflexxx, Leo Gordy, Marlon, my taxman, Bernard and XII Restaurant, Olan, Fox, Ricky Seafers, Sam Foster, Shawanna and Angie, Tomoni, Sadae and Bay Bay, Mattie Reed, Thomas "TC" Dunn, Michael Stanley Bey, and all the new friends I've met thus far and in my future. If I left anyone out, please remember that you are special, too.

Check me out at:
www.facebook.com/bigmoneyjames
www.youtube.com/mygirlgotagirlbook
www.youtube.com/jamestannerfilms
www.parkbenckentertainment.weebly.com

You can also email me at investors4film@yahoo.com.

My Girl

Got a

Girlfriend 2

Chapter 1

KEEP A MARK IN THE DARK

Dad always said fools rush in where angels fear to tread. Ace Spinner was my dad's name and running con was his game. My dad was one of the best con artists that Washington, DC had ever seen.

"Running con is an art, sweetheart. You have con men that make the game look ugly, and you have the con artists who think big and have class about how they operate and run their con. Always remember, the bigger the take, the higher the risk," he explained to me.

In the con game, we use different names to describe our victims. Dad gave me the rules to the con game:

Rule #1 - The name of your victim is always called a "mark". Always keep them unconscious and confused about your motives or intentions. Make them think and feel that everything you're saying to them is true by creating the fantasy they want or dream of, while it's really all an illusion. Drill your mark, meaning ask your mark personal questions about themselves so you'll know everything about them to run your con. This method is used by pimps as they bring a hoe into their stable. It's called breaking a hoe.

Rule #2 - A lie is the biggest part of the con game. Always make yourself look more important than you really are. Always tell your mark something different and confusing when telling them your lies, especially when you're leading them on with a bunch of promises.

Dad schooled me to these rules while standing in front of a mirror tying his necktie. I was around six years old when my dad began teaching me the con game. He taught me that anything in the world worth doing is worth doing well. Practice makes perfect; there's no doubt about it.

Throughout my childhood, Dad took me around the world with him as he pulled off his con jobs during his journeys. Either he pick-pocketed at a major convention, cashed bad checks he created from a Fortune 500 company's account, sold whores some game, or just conned anyone out of some major shit with his million promises. In one fashion or another, Dad was a player that couldn't be stopped.

My father partnered with two other players: Kidd Twist and Suitcase Murphy. They were all partners in the underworld of con. They studied books and literature on the confidence game like a person studying to get a Master's or a Ph.D. Dad always said, "Know the game, play it well, and have fun with it."

Like most little girls, I loved my father. He meant the world to me. In my eyes, Ace Spinner could do no wrong. Before my mother left us for another woman, she always had something negative to say about him.

"Your father ain't shit! With his slick, stealing, stankin' ass," she often said.

As I grew older, I understood her way of thinking. I began to understand she was jealous of him. My father was a very handsome, intelligent man, who was well groomed, respected, and liked by many people. Although he was part of the underworld and that secret society, he maintained an upper middleclass type of lifestyle. We lived in a five-hundred-thousand-dollar home. He drove a Mercedes Benz and paid my way through college.

At the age of ten, Dad asked me questions about life on a daily basis. He would say, "Envy, what is this world about? What's life about?"

He told me many things about life and this world, and he

9

expected me to remember everything he told me and why.

"There are rules; there are parameters. What do they mean to you? How do you play the game?" he would ask.

I responded back with everything I knew at the time.

"The world is about making moves to become rich and successful. Life's about being conscious of another person's ignorance and capitalizing on the inconvenience of others, whether it is their education level, financial status, or their mental incapacities. The game is played strictly on your understanding, your knowledge, and the role you play on your mark," I recited back, being only ten years old yet mature for my age.

While going to school and playing with other kids in my neighborhood, I didn't think like the average ten-year-old. It was all about power and practicing the confidence game on each and every kid I came in contact with.

One day, the bell rang for recess. My two female friends, Bossy and Lying Lyn, and I started eating our lunch right out of our lunch bags as we headed toward the playground. We saw this new kid who just entered our school. In fact, he was assigned to our class. I watched him closely and could clearly see that his parents had access to a lot of cash.

"Hey, what's your name?" I asked while walking up to the new kid.

"My name is Jerry," he replied.

I was determined to learn as much as I could about him. So, I started to drill him with countless questions.

"So where are you from, Jerry? Are your parents doctors or something? How much money do your parents give you for lunch every day?"

Just as my dad taught me, I drilled my mark for any and all information about himself because I could use that information for running cons, whether short or long, in whatever way I wanted to play it.

During the rest of the recess hour, Jerry told me as much as I asked at that time, but there was much more to find out. During the next few weeks, I hung out a lot at Jerry's house. His parents even had me stay for dinner on many of those nights.

It appeared to me that Jerry had the perfect family. His mother and father were African American and with light-skin complexions. Jerry's father, Mr. Sanders, stood about six feet tall and weighed about two hundred and fifty-five pounds. He had pretty, curly black hair with a short, trimmed beard. Mr. Sanders wore a nice expensive suit and tie each day I saw him. Mrs. Sanders dressed nicely in skirt suits and carried a briefcase every day like her husband. She stood about five-feet, four-inches, weighed approximately one hundred and twenty-five pounds, and had long black hair. The two carried briefcases every day, maintaining business-like appearances.

Once while drilling Mr. and Mrs. Sanders with numerous questions, they shared how they made a living. I learned Mr. Sanders bought and sold stocks on Wall Street, while Mrs. Sanders ran their real estate business.

One day, Mrs. Sanders decided to let me ride with her to Safeway. She had just finished having a big argument with Mr. Sanders. I think she caught him cheating with another bitch on his job or getting some head from the office manager. I listened while Mrs. Sanders went on and on over the telephone with her best friend Nicole.

"I caught the son of a bitch again, Nicole. The dirty dick motherfucker! My husband has to be the dumbest man on the fuckin' earth. I want out of this shit. I can't take it anymore. I try to do all the right things and this is the shit I get...in a marriage just to be cheated on. Fuck this shit. It's all about me now."

I tried to comfort Mrs. Sanders while helping her with the bags of groceries into their five-bedroom home. Just as we reached the kitchen area, we saw Mr. Sanders standing in the middle of the floor drinking a can of Pepsi.

"Bitch, let me tell you one motherfuckin' thing. I run the show in this house, and if you don't like the way I do things here, get your things and move the fuck out," Mr. Sanders said, then gulped the rest of the soda down his throat.

Mrs. Sanders slammed down the bags on a small table in the corner and started to cry as she walked swiftly to the living room to sit on the couch. She continued crying as she covered her face with both hands. After hearing the things that went on with her marriage, I felt sorry for her, but I was a child. What the hell did I know?

I decided I would go in the living room with Mrs. Sanders and rub her back as she released her inner pain through her tears.

My father always told me that touching and hugging a person means so much but is often underestimated. My father also told me that his father bought him any and everything, when the one thing he wanted most from him was a hug— something his dad would never do.

When I saw the relationship Mr. and Mrs. Sanders shared and how Mr. Sanders treated Mrs. Sanders, I clearly understood that love and happily-ever-after were dreams that can only be sold to square motherfuckers, as Daddy said. From that day forward, I looked at people differently. As a matter of fact, I looked at life differently.

I came to the conclusion that no one wants to feel like shit. Low self-esteem is the one thing that goes hand-in-hand with the acceptance of being treated poorly, and I refused to feel that way. Pay attention to how someone treats you on a daily basis, and you'll realize just how important you really are to the ones who say you're special.

Chapter 2

PRACTICE MAKES PERMANENT

"Con is the first profession, even before prostitution," Dad told me. "The Devil was the first one to con us thousands of years ago, and he's still conning us today."

One hot summer day, Dad took me to the National Zoo in upper Northwest Washington, DC. He put me on his back as we walked through the zoo looking for marks to pick their pockets. We saw an older white man who looked to be in his mid to late 60's. My dad bumped my foot against the old man's back. When the old guy turned and looked at us, it seemed to him that it was an innocent mistake. However, it was the beginning of a long day of work, with him being our first take of the day.

As Dad moved in to take the wallet, I got off his back.

Once a mark's wallet is taken, it cannot be held too long. It has to be dumped off to a partner as soon as possible. That way, if the police caught up to us, the evidence would be long gone. With that being said, Dad quickly handed me the wallet, and I headed for the popcorn stand near the souvenir shop where we would always meet after he clipped a mark for their wallets.

We clipped twelve people for their wallets at the zoo that day. Hours passed, and it was time to make our way home. I had school the next day, and Dad was very serious about my education. He always said if I have a good education, I could set up a mark for a big take, and when the con is over, I could go back to living my regular life until the next take. As a little girl being turned out in the con game, that made a lot of sense to me.

The next day after school, Dad took me shopping. He told me every good woman should be spoiled and taken care of well. Even though I was only about ten, Dad bought me expensive jewelry, clothes, and all kinds of gifts. If I were old enough, he would have purchased the car of my dreams.

"It's about expectations. Always remember that people must meet a certain expectation to be in your circle," Dad said as he handed me money from one of the wallets he lifted out of a man's pocket a few days earlier. "Whatever you're good at, you must practice it on a daily basis, because practice makes permanent."

A few days later, I decided to execute everything I had learned from Dad thus far. I started bringing my teacher, Ms. Brock, a juicy red apple every day to gain her confidence and have her believe I was a good student. Weeks passed, and just as I planned, I became the teacher's pet.

Dad always said never look like what you are. If you're a killer, never look like one; if you're a drug dealer, never look like one; and if you're a con artist, never look like one. It's a mental thing. Dress and act totally the opposite. One man with a suit and briefcase can take more than five hundred men with guns.

Ms. Brock moved my desk right next to hers and had me pass out paperwork to the students, in addition to helping with other classroom assignments. Her trust was just what I needed, and it made things so easy to pull off.

I began to steal money from the bake-off where students purchased cupcakes, cookies, ice cream, sweet potato pies, and other sweets. Ms. Brock placed the money in her desk during the lunch hour when the students from other classrooms came by to buy the junk food items. One of the first things I learned from my dad was to never take everything. Dad always said a con man that takes everything is what makes the con game ugly. The skilled con artist won't do that because it would make the risk high and bring the police. Plus, you might need to go back another day and steal from the pot again. Never make your take noticeable.

Years passed, and before we knew it, I was in high school. My mental con game was so strong that I had the whole school chasing me, both male and female. By this time, I realized I didn't like men. I was on pussy harder than a motherfucker, but I will admit that I played a lot of the males in the school. I made them think I liked men. I got a lot of money and gifts out of them fools, but they never got the chance to smell my pussy.

As for the females, I fucked a lot of them hoes, and that's real talk. I had no problem sharing my wealth with the ladies in order to get my freak on. I licked a lot of pussies in high school, and I was fucked, sucked, and licked by females just as much. One thing about me, I believed a bitch had to be on lock mentally, physically, and financially. Always play mind games and put your best skull game down. Skull game means to get the bitch's mind. Get in her head. Once you get her jumping through hoops to stay in your frame, you got her just where you want her. I ran a lot of game to keep money in my pocket. I sold bitches dreams that you couldn't imagine. It was all about getting them to believe I could make them rich and famous in the entertainment business.

I met Kim and Lisa, two young, beautiful girls in my school who wanted to become successful actresses. This was my chance to run some major game on them whores. So, I made my way up to Howard University's communications building to the film department. I met several students who were film majors and had to do a few class projects. We got acquainted, and I ended up forming a good friendship with them. I waited until the time was right and then took Kim and Lisa to audition for a couple small roles in the film project. I told Kim and Lisa not to say too much. Other than them doing their lines for the screenplay, I did all the talking. Lisa and Kim really did well as they auditioned for the film. As a matter of fact, they both got the roles.

A couple days later, I sat down with them to explain I would be opening a modeling agency and wanted them to be the first two models to represent my company. I decided to have them meet me at XII Restaurant and Lounge on 12th & H Streets Northeast.

I sat at the bar talking to a close friend of my father's, Kid Twist, when they walked in. I told him about this long con that I planned to run in the film game and how I would need him to convince the new marks I had lined up for a take of a hundred thousand dollars. As the girls approached, I ended the conversation, telling Kid Twist I would talk to him more about it later.

"Hey, girls," I said as Lisa and Kim walked over to the bar where Kid Twist and I sat.

"Hello, Envy," Kim said while walking over to hug me.

"Hey, Lisa. Looking sexy as ever," I said as Lisa hugged me and kissed my right cheek.

Lisa was a hot redbone who stood about five-foot-six and weighed one hundred and forty-five pounds. Kim, on the other hand, was a sexy, brown-skinned young woman that stood about five-foot-eleven, one hundred and sixty pounds. Any lesbian woman would love to stick her tongue into either one of them.

Kim's ass was so fuckin' phat and soft that if you were to fuck her from the back, her ass cheeks would probably ripple like the waves of the ocean. I hadn't fucked her yet, but I saw her in a bathing suit. So, I imagined what it would look like with a nine-inch dildo strap-on banging that ass from the back. If you ever fucked a woman from the back with a nine-inch dildo, then you know exactly what I'm talking about.

As we sat there, I talked to the girls about the price I charged to be with my agency. Even though it was a short con, I charged them bitches five hundred dollars apiece to be with my new modeling agency and entertainment group.

Pussy Bumpin' Entertainment was my new company, and I was ready to get paid off these bitches.

Chapter 3

NEVER LOOK LIKE WHAT YOU ARE

In the con game, they say a man that wears a suit and carries a briefcase can steal more money than five hundred men with guns. Whatever your con is, never look like what you are. If you do, it will raise suspicion in your mark and your con will be revealed. If you're trying to play a sucker for their money, you must look like you have money.

I was out one night promoting my new company, Pussy Bumpin' Entertainment. As I stood in front of Love Nightclub, I heard someone yelling out behind me.

"Hello, sexy momma. Sexy momma, how are you?" the accented voice called out.

When I turned around, there stood a handsome, clean-cut

man. He motioned with his hand for me to come to him. As I walked toward him, I could clearly see he was from another country. Although a foreigner, he was one dude that I thought would fit well into my future plans.

"Hello, young lady. My name is Palm Beach Fred. How are you?"

"I'm Envy. How are you, Palm Beach Fred?" I replied as we shook hands.

"I couldn't help but to notice your beauty when I saw you walk up. I said to myself, 'I need to know this woman'," Palm Beach Fred said softly while looking me straight in the eyes.

"And why do you need to know me?" I asked.

"Well, I'm a very rich man in search of happiness. Maybe you can help me," Palm Beach Fred spoke softly in my left ear.

I quickly saw an obstacle that I could turn into an opportunity, just as any player or con artist should do. Dreams can't be sold if the deliverer looks like a nightmare. Dad always said you can't talk to people about making money if you don't look like money. So, my first move on Fred was to take an application out on him, which meant listening and finding out what he had and what he was into.

Palm Beach Fred and I exchanged contact information. I

gave him my business card and he gave me his. We talked for a while longer; then I stepped off and set up another day and time for us to meet up.

I went home, ran my bath, added some bubbles, and lowered my body into the nice, warm water to relax. Resting my head on an air pillow, I closed my eyes. All I could think of was Palm Beach Fred telling me how he was a very rich man. Well, if Fred was indeed a very rich man, I had the right plot to take him for a large amount of cash.

After I got out the tub and dried off, I sipped on some wine before calling it a night.

*****

Early the next morning, I got a call from Palm Beach Fred. He asked me to meet up with him in Georgetown at his restaurant. I met with him about 2:15 p.m., and we talked about many things. Fred was interested in me in a sexual way, but if I told him that I was only interested in women, my plot would be fucked up. Knowing this, I planned step number two, mentally seducing that motherfucker to get money out of his ass.

Palm Beach Fred went on to tell me that he was Cuban and did a lot of business in Miami. In fact, he told me that he owned four hotels and eleven clothing stores all located in Palm Beach, Florida. I shared with Fred about Pussy Bumpin' Entertainment and my vision. I told him that I wanted to shoot an all-lesbian porno film with the hottest females I could find.

As I sat at the table, Fred leaned in closer to me and said, "If you want to shoot a porno flick, I would love to finance the film project for you."

I nodded. "Yes, Fred. I have a lot of girls that are ready and willing to be in the film. Maybe you should meet some of the girls I have in mind."

A couple hours later, I decided to talk with some females I met at a lesbian club in Baltimore. I began my search for the finest women that I could ever meet. I handed out flyers, which included my cell phone number, at the lesbian clubs about my first porno film. As quickly as I put the flyers in the ladies' hands, I received phone calls.

A few weeks later, I held a casting call and cast six females: three dominant and three feminine (fems). Sabrina, Sally, and Wendy were my femmes. I gave Sabrina the name Sweet Cheeks. The brown-skinned beauty stood five-feet, six-inches and her ass was right. Her measurements were 36-24-42, a shape that any dominate woman would want to stick her dick inside. Sally, who would be known as Nasty because

26

of her freakiness, was my small-town, white bitch. Her short five-foot-four frame, beautiful face, 34-26-38 shape, and blonde hair made her an obvious choice. My third fem, Wendy, was Hispanic. I named her Bubbles for the fatty that she carried around. She was the perfect fit for the sex-filled porno flicks I was about to shoot because most Spanish women are some freaky-ass bitches.

Dee Dee, Charnika, and Moka were my doms. All three were some freaky, strap-on-dildo fucking dykes that loved to eat, suck, or fuck a horny pussy. At about five-foot-eight and a hundred and thirty pounds, Dee Dee was dark skinned and wore a twelve-inch strap-on dildo at all times. Charnika was five-foot-seven, one hundred and forty-five pounds, and loved to fuck a woman until she had no more love juices to release. Moka was double the pleasure, a real pussy licker with a big, black dick. She loved to suck a woman's hole while a woman sucked on her long pole.

She Bust My Pussy was ready to be filmed. I had all the girls do a photo shoot and had my graphic artist put the front cover together so I could promote the film with flyers and large posters all around the Washington, DC area. I went to every strip club, lesbian club, mom and pop store, nail shop, beauty salon, sex toy store, magazine stand – wherever I could promote it.

Palm Beach Fred called me on a Thursday night and asked me how everything was going. When I informed him that I was ready for the first round of funds for the film, he told me that I could come and get the money first thing in the morning. After he said that, I immediately had my girlfriend to draw up a phony film-financing contract that stated Fred would finance the film and that we would split the profits. Since I never told Fred my real name, I used a fictitious first and last name on the contract. I had already told Fred that I needed him to give me cash money, no checks. Dad said to never leave a paper trail. Always have your mark give you straight cash because it can't be traced.

I met up with Fred Friday morning about ten o'clock at his restaurant. I had been sitting at a table near the front window for about fifteen minutes before Fred walked in carrying a brown Louis Vuitton suitcase. He sat the suitcase on the table, bent over, and kissed the side of my face.

"Are you ready to be a rich and famous lady, Envy?" Fred asked while opening the suitcase. "Here's one hundred thousand dollars cash to start the process, and if you need more, just let me know," he whispered.

I looked at the money and instantly came in my underwear. Not bad for my first big scam.

Fred closed the suitcase and pushed it over to my side of

the table. I had to remember that patience is important in the con game; haste arouses suspicion. Mentally, I had to act as if the money wasn't there; play it smooth all the way to the end. I told him if all continued to go well, I would love to pitch a reality show to the networks down the line. Fred definitely counted himself in with my future endeavors, and I was glad to have him aboard.

Later that evening, I hired an all-lesbian film crew and a director with over two hundred porn films attached to her name. From what I heard, Tibby, the director, made a lot of money and had a great name as a director in the business. Tibby told me that she had been a porn star herself back in the day and had done a lot of fucking in her time.

That Monday, the director, film crew, and I met up at Uno's at Union Station.

"The only types of films I've ever been in were lesbian porno films, and I loved every bit of it," Tibby shared as she gazed into my eyes.

To be honest, I found Tibby to be very sexy, and I was a bit turned on at the idea of us working together.

"I kinda figured that, but I didn't want to ask you," I replied.

"Why not? This is your project. Never be uncomfortable with asking a question," Tibby said.

"Well, I don't have a problem with asking a question at all. I just had a specific time when I would've asked you that question," I said, putting my hand on her shoulder.

As we sat, Carmon, the light technician, stood up from the round table we were sitting at and said, "During Gay Pride, this film will sell out immediately."

"Without a doubt, this will sell everywhere it goes. There's nothing like seeing a woman get fucked by another woman. The name of this film makes me wet already," Natalie, my sound engineer, said.

"Well, I'm ready to start filming. When is the potential shoot date?" the camera operator, Sarah, asked.

"That's a good question. When would you like to start shooting the film, Envy?" Tibby asked me as I sipped my water the waitress put on the table.

"I want to start shooting the film as soon as possible. Can we start next week?" I asked everyone at the table.

Everyone's schedule was free, so I called Bubbles, Sweet Cheeks, Nasty, Dee Dee, Charnika, and Moka, and told them that we would start shooting the film that Wednesday the following week.

Chapter 4

LIGHTS, CAMERA, AND ASS IN THE AIR

The entire cast and crew met me at one of Fred's eight-bedroom homes in Fort Washington, Maryland. I didn't have a slate person or a shot list person, so I called Kim and Lisa to help out on the set. Once the crew set up for the first scene, we were ready to start filming. The first scene we chose to shoot was Sweet Cheeks and Dee Dee. After everyone was in position, we began shooting.

"Quiet on the set. Tape rolling and action!" Kim yelled as she snapped the arm of the slate.

Dee Dee lay in the center of a king-sized bed, poured baby oil in her hand, and started slowly stroking a strap-on dildo.

Then she looked into the camera and said, "Hey, this is

your girl Dee Dee. As you can see, I'm stroking my big, long dick. I'm waiting for a fine-ass woman to come over and let me fuck her brains out. If you'd like to get fucked, just come over and we can fuck all night long."

Sweet Cheeks knocked on the bedroom door.

"The door is open," Dee Dee yelled. "Come on in."

Sweet Cheeks walked into the bedroom nude, sat on the bed, and took over stroking the long, black dildo. Dee Dee leaned up and tongue kissed Sweet Cheeks. They separated and Sweet Cheeks moved to Dee Dee's hard nipples, caressing them with her mouth. She slid her body on top of Dee Dee and positioned the dick inside her. She slowly moved her body, the dick entering and exiting her.

"Oh, this dick is so hard in my pussy," Sweet Cheeks moaned. "It feels so good deep up in my stomach. Oh shit, I'm going to cum hard on this dick, Dee Dee. I'm beginning to see stars, boo. Beat this pussy up, damn it! Make my stomach hurt, damn it!"

Dee Dee pumped harder as Sweet Cheeks rode her. Then Dee Dee flipped her over and placed her on all fours. She put baby oil on the dick and poured some between Sweet Cheeks' ass before sliding the dildo in.

"Oh shit, that dick feels so good in my ass. Damn, damn, damn! Feels like my ass is splitting, boo. Keep it in there, though! Damn, that hard dick in my ass is good! Fuck my ass harder. Harder, boo, harder. I want my ass to hurt."

Dee Dee pounded Sweet Cheeks' ass for twenty minutes straight before Sweet Cheeks pulled the hard dildo out her ass.

"Eat my pussy, bitch," she told Dee Dee.

Doing as told, Dee Dee licked Sweet Cheeks' clit and sucked her pussy lips. Sweet Cheeks opened her legs, and Dee Dee stuck her middle finger into her pussy while continuing to lick her pussy and ass. Sweet Cheeks enjoyed another twenty-five minutes of head before she began to cum.

"Oh shit, that's some good-ass tongue you got. Keep it right there. I'm about to cum. Oh, shit! Oh shit! Oh shit! Look at this white cum coming out my pussy," Sweet Cheeks yelled.

Shortly after Sweet Cheek reached her orgasm, the director yelled, "Cut! That's a wrap. Let's get ready for scene two!"

Nasty and Charnika were up next. Tibby and two female film crewmembers stood to the side of the room while the set designer prepared the room for the next scene.

"I believe this scene should be an innocent white schoolgirl looking for some special attention from a naughty lesbian friend," Tibby suggested as she looked at a TV monitor. "Okay, Nasty, in this scene, I want you to pick up the telephone and call Charnika. Tell her that you're in need of some hardcore lesbian lovemaking. Charnika, you're going to be on the outside of the door knocking as she calls. Okay, quiet on the set. Tape rolling and action!"

Nasty sat on the side of the bed with not a stitch of clothing on. She slid a magnum-sized condom on a huge cucumber and then inserted the big, thick, twelve-inch vegetable in her tight vagina.

"Oh, this is a big piece of vegetable I'm stickin' in and out of my wet, horny pussy," Nasty said as she picked up her cell phone and dialed Charnika to come in the room.

Nasty held the cell phone up to her ear as she listened to each ring.

Charnika answered the phone. "Hey, sweetheart, I was just thinking about you. I want to come over and lick your sweet pussy lips until you cum," Charnika said.

"Oh, that would be so damn nice. Come suck my clit like you suck a vanilla milkshake through a straw," Nasty moaned.

Charnika opened the room door and walked over to the bed, where she kneeled down and started licking on Nasty's clit and pussy lips. From one side to the other, she went up and down on Nasty's sweet, wet pussy.

"Get on your knees. I want to lick it from the back," Charnika said.

Once Nasty was in position, Charnika started tonguing her ass.

"Oh, that feels so damn good! Spit on my ass, baby. Spit on my asshole and stick that cucumber inside my tight, little asshole. When you fuck with my ass, it makes me cum so hard. Now take your pants off, sweetie," Nasty moaned.

After Charnika took off her pants and underwear, Nasty licked on Charnika's clit. Nasty pushed the layer of skin back and sucked and licked Charnika's clitoris until Charnika exploded. Charnika held Nasty's head with both hands as her body shook.

"Nasty, you got some good-ass head. Stick that tongue up in my pussy until I cum in your mouth. Yeah, that's it. That's it. Right there! Keep that wet tongue right there, baby," Charnika groaned.

Twenty-five minutes later, Charnika screamed, "Damn, I'm cummin'; I'm cummin'. Damn, boo, I'm cummin' all in your mouth."

As Charnika bust her nut in Nasty's mouth, Nasty fucked herself with the thick, long cucumber. She used the cucumber like she had a twelve-inch dildo.

"I love getting fucked by a real lesbian. I love the hard

35

dick them dyke bitches slammed up in my asshole. I love it!" Nasty moaned.

"Cut! I need a close up on her when she talks like that. Nasty, look in the camera when you talk freaky like that," Tibby yelled.

Just as we were about to wrap up that scene, Fred called.

"Hello. Fred?"

"Hey, sweetheart, how are things going on the set?" he asked.

"Everything is going well. We're about to finish up the second scene. We have one more scene to shoot before the film will be ready for editing," I told Fred as I stood outside of the room we were filming in.

"That's great, Envy. You're going to be a star someday. You'll be rich and famous. Just don't forget about the little people like me," Fred said.

We laughed.

"Now, Fred, how could I do that? You're the rich and famous person. Without you, this film wouldn't be possible," I whispered.

It was obvious that Fred was trying to fuck me, which wasn't going to happen. I wasn't into men; I considered myself a lesbian, not bisexual. At some point, I knew I would have to go and talk to my dad about Fred. He would be the right person to get the proper advice from on how to handle the situation.

"Well, I'm about to take a trip to Columbia for some important business. You need anything before I leave?" he asked.

"No, not right now. My focus is on this film. I want to make sure I do my best," I replied.

As a con artist, I knew I had to keep Palm Beach Fred fooled with confidence. The first rule in con is to lie and keep your mark fooled by having them put all their confidence in you. Always let your mark make the last decision, as if they're in control. So, I knew to keep Fred fooled. That way, I could take him for his money slowly.

"Envy, you're a very beautiful woman. Make sure you live up to the expectation that a woman on your level would. I want to make you famous," Fred said.

"I will, Fred. That's my dream—to be rich. Well, I'm going back to the set. I think they're waiting on me to come back before they start filming," I told him.

"Enjoy filming," Fred said before I hung up to return to the set.

"Okay, we're going to get this cum shot. Then we'll be done with this scene. Everybody get in place and let's finish up. Quiet on the set. Tape rolling and action!" Kim yelled.

Charnika fucked Nasty with the cucumber and licked her pussy as she stuck the thick, long vegetable in and out of her pussy. Fifteen minutes later, Nasty had the biggest orgasm of her life. She came so hard that she shook uncontrollably. We thought she was having a heart attack or something, but she finally calmed down.

As we prepared for the last scene with Moka and Bubbles, I watched Nasty from a distance. I couldn't help but to stare at her pretty pink pussy. I always wanted to fuck a white girl.

After walking over to her, I said, "I enjoyed watching you get fucked with the cucumber. I just wished it was me who had the chance to suck and fuck your pussy."

Nasty whispered in my ear, "Envy, you must have read my mind. I want you to fuck me so bad. I want to lick your ass as soon as you get out of the shower, honey."

"We will get together later and set up a day and time when we can meet and have a good fucking, sucking time," I said.

We finally set up for the last scene where Moka and Bubbles would fuck on the kitchen floor. Bubbles started the scene wearing some black high heel stilettos and a very short skirt with no underwear. Her titties hung free as she stood with her back against the wall and playing with her pussy. Moka walked into the frame, got on her knees, and licked

Bubbles' clit as she stood with her legs wide open.

"Lick this pussy, boo. Lick this pussy like you want me to cum, baby," Bubbles moaned while humping Moka's mouth.

Moka sucked and licked on Bubbles' pussy for twenty-five minutes before she reached up, opened the freezer, and grabbed an ice cube.

"Get down on all fours," Moka softly said.

Bubbles got on her hands and knees. Moka put the ice cube in her mouth, spread Bubbles' ass cheeks, and proceeded to lick her brown asshole.

"Oooh, oooh, oooh...my pussy is so wet, sweetheart. I love the way you suck me. My ass...my ass...my asshole feels like it's cumming."

Moka made Bubble cum about three times before the director yelled cut. I got so excited that it seemed like my asshole was cumming, too. We all knew one couldn't cum from their butthole, but the sensation I experienced came as close to the feeling of an orgasm as it could.

With the last scene finished, the film went straight to editing. About three weeks later, the master copy of the film was finished. Once it was packaged and wrapped, we sent copies to the distributors to be sold to the retailers. I talked to Fred and told him the good news.

"The film is finished, Fred. We finished the film, and it's

being pushed to the stores as we speak," I told him.

"That's great, Envy! I told you, baby. You're gonna be a star. We need to celebrate," Fred said.

I told Fred that I spent the entire budget on the film, and he went for the okie doke. I told him a boldface lie. In actuality, Fred gave me one hundred thousand dollars to shoot the film, but I only spent ten thousand dollars to put everything together. The remaining ninety thousand dollars went in my pocket. *Fuck 'em!* I created all types of receipts for that fool to make it look like I spent the money for the reason it was given to me, but that was just to make it look good. Ladies, if you know how to run game, then you know what I'm talking about. It's about working a motherfucker for all that you can get them for, and don't forget it. If done right, running game can be very profitable.

Chapter 5

ART FOR THE TAKING

Not having any emotional attachments or inner feelings for someone saved me a lot of heartaches and headaches. It helped me to remember that their love for me made it easy to hustle them out of whatever I was after. It all came down to how much I could convince them that I loved them without them seeing that I was playing them like a game of Monopoly. I always manipulated them with the things that made them weak, but I restrained from having inner feelings, even if I had a lot of sex. I was direct and knew I was the manager. It was my show. I always looked like money, kept my fronts up well, and was always seen in nice clothes, cars, and jewelry. I kept money, even if I had to pull out a Michigan bank roll. I faked them out as long as I could, because they were very easy to control. I had them jumping through hoops to stay in my life, and they bought time with any and all they had. I was a boss player, too, and players like me played all day, every day.

Although I was a lesbian, I played on men, women, and even kids. I had no cut card. That may have made me a dirty bitch, true. But, remember, practice makes permanent.

I ran into a lesbian friend named Pink Lips. She sounded like a black girl when she talked, but she was a slender white girl with long blonde hair. She was one hell of an art thief. I mean, this broad could steal the most expensive painting right off a museum wall. Alarms couldn't stop this bitch! Pink Lips was one bitch museums didn't want to see coming.

I walked into a nearby beauty salon in upper Georgetown and actually bumped right into her as she was coming out.

"Oh, excuse me," Pink Lips said as her shoulder hit me dead center in my chest.

"No, excuse me, miss," I responded, then realized who it was that had bumped into me. "Pink Lips? How are you, girl?" I asked.

"Envy, girl, how in the hell are you?"

We hugged and kissed each other on the side of the face. We ended up talking for hours, and before we knew it, the damn beauty salon was closing for the night. I didn't trip about not getting my hair done, though, because it turned out to be a great opportunity seeing Pink Lips. We set up shop and planned our first hustle since our last a few years back.

"I've been looking for a few auctions where they sell some very old paintings, like "Guernica" by Pablo Picasso, and "The Scream" finished in 1893, "The Sick Child" finished in 1885, and "Madonna" finished in 1895, all three painted by Edvard Munch. His paintings are almost as famous as the Mona Lisa painting," Pink Lips said quietly while looking around. "Those paintings sell for millions. I mean, tens and hundreds of millions of dollars," Pink Lips added as she searched through the *Washington Post* newspaper.

She knew what she was talking about, because she had taken a few million-dollar paintings on several occasions.

After days and hours of searching through newspapers and magazines, Pink Lips finally found an auction that would be selling of expensive paintings. We decided to go to The Gallery at East 71st Street at the corner of Madison Avenue in New York City. We rented a car and headed to the Big Apple. Pink Lips was out for major takes, and I was right there with her. We knew we may have to play the ole catch and cap role, which meant I would catch the mark and convince him to believe we were buyers of antique paintings. Then I would bring the unsuspecting victim to Pink Lips so she could knock them off for the painting.

We drove for five hours and arrived in the big city of dreams about one o'clock that afternoon. Time was of the essence. We got there just as the art gallery was about to open. We had to get into our roles as expensive art buyers and start the search for our first rich-ass victim.

After paying the admission fee to get into the auction, Pink Lips and I sat next to each other in the second row toward the front. The large exhibit room was jammed packed with many people, all of them rich. I even spotted three famous people waiting to buy some expensive art, but I won't call any names. A bitch ain't trying to get sued, you hear me?

As the employees at The Gallery brought out the expensive paintings, people waved their numbered auction cards in the air as part of the bidding process. The bidding started at seven hundred and fifty thousand dollars for the first painting.

"Wow, seven hundred and fifty thousand dollars? Damn," I whispered in Pink Lips' ear.

At that point, I knew life was going to be bigger than I could ever imagine. Dad had prepared me for the stage, and I was ready to perform.

After about an hour of watching the rich and famous purchase the paintings, people loosened up a bit and talked to us while bidding on the merchandise. I talked and joked with an old white couple sitting directly beside me. The wife said her name was Mildred, and her husband introduced himself as Bernard. I told them that my name was Jemeka, and I introduced Pink Lips to them as Marlene. We all shook hands, and then they went on to tell us about the paintings they bought in the past and what they planned to accomplish at the gallery.

Everything went the way I thought it would. The longer we kept the rich, old couple sharing their personal business with us, the more convinced I was that our payday would be the ultimate satisfaction.

Bernard asked us if we'd like a bottle of water since he was on his way to get a few bottles for him and his wife. I decided to go with him over to the concession stand.

When Bernard handed me about four bottles of water, I looked him in the eyes and said, "Thank you. Here's twenty dollars."

"No, no, this is my treat. Besides, I like to take care of my friends."

When Bernard said that, I didn't know if he was getting fresh with me or not, but I played past it.

As he bent down to get two more bottles of water out of an ice cooler, I clipped him for his wallet. It's hard for a con artist to let an opportunity get by, especially when you have experience playing the cannon, too. In case you don't know what playing the cannon means, it's when you pick a person for their wallet.

When Bernard and I got back to our seats, people were bidding like crazy. After sitting down next to Pink Lips, she informed me that Mildred told her that they were owners of one of the largest fur companies in the United States, and she asked that we attend some of the International Fur Trade Federation shows. They gave us business cards with all the information we needed to know, and since I had clipped Bernard for his wallet, I now knew where they laid their fuckin' heads at night.

As we sat and watched many of the expensive paintings being auctioned off, we clearly saw the type of crowd we needed to surround ourselves with. Back in the hood, they have no understanding of stepping out of that circle. All they see is what they will ever be.

Mildred and Bernard ending up winning a bid for a painting worth more than five hundred thousand dollars. Pink Lips and I made eye contact that said it was time to go to work on these motherfuckers.

An hour and a half later, the auction ended, and a large crowd of people were leaving. We hugged Mildred and shook

Bernard's hand. They figured we went our separate ways, but we were following them as they drove. Block after block, turn after turn, we were on their fuckin' trail.

They stopped at Junior's Restaurant at 1515 Broadway in Manhattan. We wanted to get something to eat, as well, especially having heard how good the food was at Junior's, but we could not afford to let our marks see us. So, we sat in the car and waited for about an hour and a half before we saw them get back into their car. Again, we started following them, only to end up at the Milford Hotel. As we watched from a distance as the fuckin' jerks check into the damn hotel, I had a feeling it was going to be a long night for both of us. And that it was. Pink Lips and I sat in the rental car from the time they checked into the Milford Hotel until five o'clock the next evening.

During the time we waited, it seemed like I had to piss every twenty minutes. Even worse, Pink Lips had gas and was blowin' me out in that joint. We were both hungry as hell, but with a five-hundred-thousand-dollar painting up for the take, we could not make any mistakes. Even though it was a long night, we both made it through. The next morning, Pink Lips walked to a nearby McDonald's and grabbed two Big Breakfast platters and orange juice for us.

Not long after we ate, we saw Mildred and Bernard exit

the hotel and walk to their car. We were right back on their trail again. Bernard leaned over to Mildred while she drove and gave her a kiss on the cheek. They seemed to be a very nice old couple, and they were extremely rich on top of it. They had shit that even close family would kill for.

We followed Mildred and Bernard for about an hour before they stopped at some unknown white man's house. Pink Lips and I decided we needed to get that damn painting out of their hands right the fuck then. As we watched an old elderly white man open the door of a red brick two-story house, we noticed neither Bernard nor Mildred had the painting in their hand.

Pink Lips looked at me and said, "Did you see what I saw?"

"I'm not sure. What did you see?" I replied.

"Neither of them had the painting in their hand. I think they left it in that damn car," Pink Lips softly said, then exited the car and approached theirs.

She looked back at me before opening the front driver door, which they left unlocked. How trusting are they, right? Pink Lips smiled at me, got into the car, started the engine, and pulled off. I followed her for about ten blocks. I figured she was trying to find a good place to ditch the car. Distracted by talking on her cell phone, she ran a red light. Just as I stopped at the light, a gold Crown Victoria with flashing red and blue police lights sped up behind her.

After Pink Lips pulled the car over, two Hispanic narcotic task force police officers got out and approached the driver's side of the stolen car. One police officer opened the door for Pink Lips to get out. The second officer searched the car and pulled out the painting when he opened the trunk.

I pulled over and parked the rental car, and then watched as the two officers searched the stolen car, while Pink Lips argued with them. Before she knew it, they slapped the handcuffs on her and threw her in the back of the unmarked police car.

Then, the police officer who handcuffed her grabbed the painting and walked toward my car. As the officer got closer, every bone in my body shook with fear. It seemed like he was moving in slow motion as he walked up to me.

"Excuse me, ma'am, but do you know the young lady who was driving that stolen car?" the cop asked.

"No, sir, I've never seen that lady before in my life," I said nervously.

The cop looked at me strangely for a few seconds. "Okay. It's just that you looked a little suspicious as you sat and watched us investigate the young lady and the stolen car. I apologize. You're free to leave," the cop told me, then walked away.

As the two cops pulled off with Pink Lips in the backseat, I thought to myself, *What the hell? I know she didn't just get arrested when she could have taken the painting out of their car, and we could've just driven the rental car back to Washington, DC.* I shook my head in silence while thinking about what had just happened. I just could not believe it. I found myself sitting in that very spot for three more hours with tears falling from my eyes.

Shortly after I broke out of my depressed mental state of mind, I drove to a nearby strip club called Lace at 725 7th Avenue before going back to DC. I met a few of the girls as they performed on stage. The club was so crowded that people could barely move past each other.

After about an hour, I walked over to this stripper who had the finest ass a lesbian like myself would want to see. It just so happened she had a little penis swinging from side to side, also. I put a one-hundred-dollar bill on her as she shook her soft ass all over the stage.

"What's your name, boo? And can I get your number? I want to talk you," I said calmly in her ear.

"My name is Honey Bunn, and my number is 212-555-5657. Call me tomorrow," she replied.

I walked out of the strip club, jumped into the rental, and

headed for Washington, DC. As I continued to go over the situation that happened to Pink Lips, it seemed like time flew by, because I got back to DC in no time. It took about three or four hours, but it really didn't feel like it.

I went to my father's house and talked to him about what happened to Pink Lips. Dad told me the situation did not sound right at all. I really didn't understand what he meant until I saw the news two days later. The reporter said a couple five-hundred-thousand-dollar paintings were stolen in New York City and the thieves had not been caught.

Ace Spinner called me and said he had just seen the news, and that a con artist can never consider himself to be the best until he or she can con their partner for the take. When my father told me that, I realized it was all an act. Pink Lips was not in jail, and those cops were not real cops. It was a smooth setup; that's all part of the game.

After being taken, I decided to chill and regroup.

Chapter 6

I LICKED MY WOUNDS

After I got over the shit Pink Lips did, I got back on my grind and started making moves again. I couldn't be bitter about that shit; instead, I charged it to the game. That was one big lesson to me, and I had to understand that I broke a cardinal rule: *never trust anyone or believe what they say.* The face is only the front porch of the body of lies. In other words, people hide behind their faces. One should not be fooled by the sweet words of game or by what one thinks to see. That goes for male or female, no matter the sexual preference. Be careful what you go for!

Deciding to get more aggressive in the game, I promised myself that I would squeeze every head I came in contact with like a motherfuckin' lemon. It wasn't hard for me; I simply looked at it like business. I had to charge shit to the game and so would my marks. If I could take a friend for what I could take them for, then it was fair game. So-called friends lie, cheat, and steal from each other anyway, so why should I treat my friends differently?

I needed to mix my profession as a con artist with a profession in the mainstream of society, so I decided to get a motherfuckin' job. I figured I could work motherfuckers from a different angle, just like I worked a square-ass mark on the damn street.

After applying for several jobs, I got a call back from Capitol Hill Hospital on 8th Street Southeast. I started out as a data entry assistant. I mainly helped with paperwork and ran errands around the hospital. It seemed like I had the easiest job in the building. All I did was walk around, line up my marks, and fuck every down low woman I could fuck. One thing I could say about working at the hospital, getting freaky was easy. Everybody was fucking somebody or had fucked somebody in that place. There may have been a hand full of people that never fucked a co-worker, but everyone else had dropped them panties or lifted her skirt to bend over a desk somewhere in that hospital. Believe that! The hospital should be one big swinger party.

As I continued to work at the hospital, I met different

types of people on a daily basis. I met Tina, a white chick who worked in the mailroom. The bitch thought she was all that, but she looked like SpongeBob SquarePants. She fucked old men and played the relationship game on them. I respected her hustle, though, because that love shit ain't nothing but a game for those who don't know.

I met a slew of women with self-esteem on zero. Men beat them down to a no-count. I met one bitch in particular named Dayneda. This bitch was dealing with her son's father when she first started working in the hospital, but then she started fucking this dude name Rayvon a month after she learned her way around her place of employment. I figured she was a slick, Southside hood bitch that lied like there was no tomorrow.

It snowed the first year she was there, and the dude Rayvon conned the hoe like a true player. The snow reached about eighteen inches, so Dayneda had to stay at the hospital for about two days. Rayvon was a short, light-skinned dude who liked to wear cheap-ass dress suits. He was a straight bamma, but as the rule in the con game states, never look like what you are.

A suit and a briefcase works a hoe every time. Rayvon really made the hoe feel like something by paying the snow removal guys to clean the snow off her car and make her a clear pathway. It was some short game, but as Bishop Don Juan would say, "It was good game!" Dayneda was an easy hoe to fuck and really wasn't made of any substance. Rayvon fucked that hoe all over the damn hospital. He fucked her in her office, in his office, in the doctor's sleeping room, in her car, and at the hotel down the street. He wore the bitch's pussy out so much that he told people all over the hospital how the bitch rolled. The bitch went nuts when she started fuckin' the nigga.

The low self-esteem bitch thought she was hot shit, and it was nothing anyone could tell the hoe. But, just like every other poo-butt-ass hoe that meets a new dude on the job, she got tricked.

She only wanted dick in her mouth and in her ass anyway, so she only got what she was worth. I had the chance to sit down and talk with Dayneda during lunch one day, and she spilled her guts about every piece of dirt she had on everybody, telling me everything that she knew was going on in the hospital. She tried to fake like she's cool and down to earth, but the bitch was a hot bitch for real and would call the police at the drop of a hat.

"Girl, Rayvon has a big-ass dick and knows how to work it, too," Dayneda said, turning her lips up like a crackhead.

"Oh yeah? He's beating your pussy up, huh?" I said like I

was concerned, while only caring about framing the hoe and playing her for more information.

"Yeah, girl. When he's finished fucking me, I have to go take about five Advil to stop my stomach from hurting. His dick is twelve inches long and about five inches thick. I took some pictures of it with my cell phone. Girl, look," Dayneda said as she rolled her eyes down and held her stomach with her right hand.

She then pulled her cell phone out of her pocket and showed me countless pictures of Rayvon's dick.

This bitch is sick, I thought. By me being a lesbian, I felt like I was about to vomit at the sight of a man's penis.

Dayneda went on to tell me that she had worked for an airline company before she came to the hospital and how she attended many swinger parties with co-workers at Dulles Airport. I asked her had she ever been with a woman, and she didn't give me a clear direct answer. But, I could tell she was open to some hardcore female-to-female fucking.

Even though I don't like to fuck women who have sexual relations with men, I felt the need to take this bitch down for the count. All I needed to do was to wait for Rayvon to break the bitch's heart. It was something I knew about him that she didn't know. He had about ten bitches that he fucked in the hospital, and she was going to be cancelled at some point. I knew that broad wasn't on my level, and I also knew the bitch ran her mouth for the hell of it. I figured I would trick the hoe and get her to put my pussy in her mouth as soon as I caught her slipping. Once she had my pussy in her mouth, her paycheck would be mine. I heard Rayvon got paid real well. Now it was my turn.

A couple weeks passed, and Dayneda and I had been hanging out. She came over to my house for drinks; I even cooked dinner for her sometimes. I found out she had two other kids: a daughter and another son other than her youngest son. All her kids were by three different men. She was a hot mess, the type of desperate bitch that would do anything. It wasn't for me to judge her, but it was about knowing my victim and when to wait for the right time to execute my plans for her. I decided to always keep the ball in her lap. I let her do most of the talking and only spoke when I had to, making it seem like she could always talk to me. We know most of the people who tell us that bullshit ain't to be trusted, because they are quick to go tell the next person all the business. I baited her pretty good, though. She opened up a little more every day.

She told me how her mother was a crack addict and how her father shot heroin in his arm. Dayneda told me that whenever her mother came to her house, she hid her rent money and all other valuables so her mom couldn't steal them. Even the kids had to hide their shit.

"That's ridiculous! I could never imagine something like that," I softly said to her while rubbing her back.

"I can never count on my mother for anything. That crack has really fucked her up. When I was a child, she had all types of abusive men. I can remember one dude that busted out all of our windows in the apartment she was renting," Dayneda said. She began to laugh to keep from crying.

I thought to myself, *This bitch is carrying a lot of luggage in her head, and there are many more bitches out here just like her.* You got to watch out for these types of women, because they will act like they're cool, but turn out to be as crazy as a wild woman in a strait jacket sentenced to a mental ward.

I played Dayneda close. You know, the 'I'm your best friend forever' shit. I put that in her head to gain her trust. I asked Dayneda if she'd like to go to the Delta Club on Friday night with me. She told me that she had heard about the Delta Club and would love to go. To make the hood rat feel important, I called MC Lucky and had her put Dayneda and me on the guest list.

Later that week, we went out to happy hour and had more drinks while getting the chance to chill and get closer in friendship, or so she thought.

I drove my 325i BMW over to Dayneda's place about one in the morning to take her to the Delta Club to see MC Lucky, Babii, and the rest of the girls perform. As I pulled up in front of Dayneda's apartment, I saw her and a man arguing back and forth like they were about to start throwing punches. I got out the car, grabbed her, and tried to walk her away from the guy, but she was just showing out. She was all up in the man's face cursing so bad that I saw the change in the man's facial expression; it went from being surprised to getting angry.

"You're pathetic when it comes to supporting your son. You haven't bought him anything in the last two years. What kind of man are you?" Dayneda shouted, pointing her finger in his face.

"Bitch, I haven't given him shit because you been telling people lies, telling people that I don't take care of him. I been buying him clothes, shoes, Pampers, milk, and giving you money since he's been born. Because I don't want your ass, you go and make up them lies on me," the man said, while pointing his finger back in her face.

"Dayneda, come on. Let's go. I thought we were going to the Delta Club?" I yelled, holding on to her arm as we walked over to my car.

Dayneda continued to curse at the man who I believed was the father of one of her kids. I heard the man yelling out that he had bought her other kids clothes and food when he came to her apartment from time to time.

After finally getting Dayneda in my car, we were off to the club. I had the chance to talk to her about her situation with him as we headed to the club.

"He can't give me a child support check. Shit, taking care of his son is more than a pair of shoes and a few outfits here and there," she said.

"Don't you know many women out here don't get *anything* from their children's fathers? You need to be thankful he does what he can. He may need some time to get things together, you know. I believe most people need time to get on the better side of the track. Deep down in your heart, do you still have feelings for him?" I asked as we pulled up to a red stoplight at North Capital and H Street Northeast.

"Yes, I really do have feelings for him. I've asked him to come have sex with me, but he turned me down. It seems I have him in the palm of my hand sometimes, but at the same token, he'll switch up on me as fast as a racecar goes from zero to sixty," Dayneda responded, looking into my eyes.

We finally pulled up in front of the Delta Club, where I saw MC Lucky and MC Tuffy going inside. I told Dayneda that MC Lucky and MC Tuffy were the greatest MC's in the Washington/Baltimore area insofar as MC's go. I also told her that many females admired MC Lucky and loved to see her dance. MC Lucky had some haters, too, but for the most part, everyone loved her.

We parked and got out of the car.

"Envy, thanks for pulling me away from my baby's daddy and his drama. I just get tired of him bringing shoes and clothes. I want a check every month, ya heard?" Dayneda said as the security guy searched us before we walked into the club.

"I understand you, but remember that there are many women that wish their children's father would just buy things like Pampers and milk, not to mention shoes and clothes. You're blessed with that. There are a lot of women that don't get anything, and the men are working or selling drugs like a motherfucker. You're lucky," I reminded the bitch.

Some men don't give the hood rat bitches nothing and still get some head or pussy from them dumb-ass hoes. This bitch was trippin', but that's what happens when you fuck with a control freak.

We finally got into the Delta Club, and it was jammed pack with some of the finest women on the planet. The women in Washington, DC are the most beautiful women you could ever see. I saw some fine-ass women with big bubble asses. I ain't gonna lie. My mouth started to water, and my fuckin' clit got hard as a rock. I wanted a tongue on my pussy bad as a motherfucker, but I had to slow walk Dayneda. I knew she was a freak-ass broad, but I couldn't blow my cover and let the hoe know what I was after. I sorta felt like a vampire out for blood.

I want your tongue, bitch. I want your tongue, I thought, while consistently watching Dayneda's every move.

"What are you drinking?" I asked, allowing my hand to accidentally bump into her soft, round ass.

"I'll have a Grey Goose and cranberry juice," Dayneda said as her hand *accidentally* bumped the nipple of my breast.

While walking over to the bar to get the drinks, I wondered if she had bumped my nipple on purpose or not. But, I did know my heart was pumping, and I was ready to tell the hoe that I wanted her to suck my pussy.

I screamed to the bartender to get her attention.

"Hey, sexy lady, can I order some drinks?" I yelled out over the extremely loud music.

"Yes, may I help you?" the bartender asked.

"Yes, can I get two triple shots of Grey Goose and just a little bit of cranberry juice?"

"Yes, you can, dear," the cute bartender replied.

After getting the drinks, I walked over to a table Dayneda found for us to sit and chill. Women were dancing everywhere; the club was jumping with wall-to-wall honeys.

I turned my glass of Grey Goose up in the air and drank about half of the glass. Almost instantly, I started to feel the effects of the smooth vodka. You know how you suddenly get the heart of a lion when you start to feel the liquor flowing through your veins. Well, that's me when I start feeling my drink. I looked around the club feeling like I was the baddest bitch in there. I'm not the type to fight or go start shit with people. I just feel freaky, want to dance, and say what's on my mind. You know how that is, right?

Dayneda and I stood up and started dancing in front of our seats at the table. When the record by DC's own rap artist Nonchalant came on, everybody started singing the lyrics as they danced to the music. *Five o'clock in the morning, where you gonna be? Outside on the corner! You better get yo'self together...*

"I was a little girl, but I remember that song like it was yesterday," I said to Dayneda.

An hour and three drinks later, Dayneda was toasted; I mean, she was fucked up and I was about to lay it all on the table.

I put my arm around Dayneda and said, "You should stay

over my place tonight. I will take you home early in the morning."

Dayneda had some very nice lips, and I was ready to see just how good they were going to feel on my hairless pussy. Dayneda was really out of it. She was so drunk that she got up out of her seat, walked over to the stage area, and started dancing on one of the dancer's ass. The nasty way that she danced caused me to get hornier by the minute. Then one of the female security officers spoiled the fun when she politely grabbed Dayneda by the arm and escorted her back over to the table where we sat.

We sat and watched Babii come out and dance. She's so cool that she walked out onto the stage with Hot Reds and Tresha Da Body, two well-known music video models from the Washington, DC area. I saw in the *Washington Post* that they were about to sign a contract with a top-modeling agency in Hollywood, California. I was glad to see two homegirls from the DMV finally beginning to make it in the business.

Hot Reds was a light-skinned woman with long, blonde hair. Her measurements were 36-24-36 on a five-foot-eleven frame. Now Tresha Da Body had a body out of this world, and I heard her sex game was on one hundred. She was fucking this dude who worked with me at the hospital named

Big Al. He told me that he fucked her for six months on a regular basis and her slow neck was so good that she could suck a basketball through a garden hose. Tresha Da Body stood about five feet, eight inches tall and weighed about one hundred and fifty pounds, everything in all the right places.

As the two sexy models walked Babii out on stage, a song by Notorious B.I.G. started playing. Babii danced as women of all shapes and sizes threw lots of money on the stage. A few minutes later, the host counted down from ten to one, the song ended, and Babii left the stage with a backpack full of money.

Several dom and fem dancers hit the stage after Babii, and shortly after them, MC Lucky emerged from the dressing room and hit the stage. The song *One In A Million* by Aaliyah played as MC Lucky came out wearing some dark shades, an Adidas sweat suit, and tennis shoes. The jacket to the sweat suit was unzipped, allowing you to catch a view of both her large breasts. MC Lucky didn't do much dancing. She walked out, grabbed a short, brown-skinned woman who appeared to be about thirty years old, and told her to get on her knees. MC Lucky then put her pussy close to the woman's face and started to hump it.

Next, she walked over to a short, chubby female, bent the woman over a chair, and humped her ass from behind for about two minutes as the song played. Once MC Tuffy count down from ten to one, MC Lucky walked off stage with a bag full of money, also.

As everyone spilled out of the club, Dayneda and I headed for the front door, as well. When we reached my car, we noticed two young females fighting four cars over from my car, but we got into my car and kept it moving. I told Dayneda that I was going straight to my place and wanted her to come with me.

She looked at me for about thirty seconds before saying, "I hope you don't mind, but I sleep butt naked."

"Oh, that's no problem. That's what I want you to do," I replied with a smile.

Dayneda fell asleep as I drove to my place. All I could do was look at her and wonder how sex would be with her. Thirty-three minutes passed, and I was pulling up in front of my place. After waking up Dayneda, I helped her into my apartment and told her to lie on the couch while I went to the bathroom to run our bubble bath.

Once the tub was filled, I called Dayneda upstairs to the bathroom and then helped her out of her clothes and into the tub. I took off all my clothes, as well, and joined her. Horny, I immediately started sucking her breasts, sucking and licking on her nipples for about twenty minutes. She finger-fucked my pussy underwater; then she stuck two fingers in my ass while sucking on my nipples. The more she finger-fucked my asshole, the more my hairless pussy wanted her tongue.

Standing up in the tub, I positioned my pussy in front of Dayneda's face, and as if she had done this before, she licked on my clit. She licked and sucked on my clitoris while I humped her tongue very slowly.

"Oh yes, Dayneda, suck my pussy. That's it, baby. Nice and slow. Suck this pussy right. Ahhh, baby," I moaned as she viciously sucked my pussy.

Sweat rolled down my face, neck, and back as I fucked Dayneda's hot wet mouth.

"Is that pussy wet yet? Is your pussy wet and ready to cum?" Dayneda asked just as a white glob of cum skeeted out onto her long, red tongue.

As Dayneda continued sucking my pussy and finger-fucking my asshole, she swallowed the glob of cum like it was a sweet treat.

Getting out the tub, I bent over the toilet and told her to come lick my asshole. Doing as told, she licked my asshole while I played with my clit until I started cumming again.

Afterwards, we washed up and got into my king-sized bed. Reaching into my nightstand, I pulled out my twelve-inch dildo, strapped it on, and fucked Dayneda for several hours.

I beat her pussy up; it was daybreak before we stopped. We got up around one o'clock that afternoon and cooked breakfast. I wanted pancakes, scrambled eggs, and turkey link sausages with a tall glass of orange juice.

Dayneda had a hangover from drinking too much alcohol at the club, but shortly after she got some breakfast in her, she turned out to be okay.

"I need to get home to my kids. I know they're wondering where I am. Plus, I have to give my daughter some money for watching my two boys," Dayneda told me as she put her plate in the kitchen sink.

I walked over to Dayneda, grabbed her face with both hands, and kissed her straight in the mouth. I mean, I tongue kissed her like I never kissed a woman in my life.

She had sucked my pussy real good, and I wanted her and her skilled mouth in my life for a while. I just had to get this bitch to fuck with me and only me.

Chapter 7

EVERYBODY LIES;
SOME JUST LIE BETTER THAN
OTHERS

There's nothing wrong with selling a little misdirection at times. Never let anyone totally know who you really are or what to expect from you. Always keep people in the dark and remain a mystery to everyone, even family.

I was sitting at my desk at work, when my cell phone rang. On the third ring, I answered and was surprised to hear it was Palm Beach Fred. I had been trying to blow him off since I took him for the ninety grand. Just so you all can understand the lingo, blow him off means the last stage of the con once you got their money. Meaning, dismiss your mark and get the hell out of sight. But, even though I was trying to blow him off, I knew I had to do it smoothly. Therefore, I answered the phone.

"Hello, my sweet red rose. How are you doing today?" Fred asked.

"I'm fine, Fred. What's going on with you? Are you back in town?" I inquired.

Palm Beach Fred went on to tell me that his eighteen-year-old daughter would be coming in town, and he wanted to know if she could hang out with me for a few days.

"You have an eighteen-year-old daughter, Fred?"

"Yes, I do. I'll send a picture to your phone. She's a great daughter to me," Fred commented before hanging up.

A few minutes later, I received a text from Fred, and it was a picture of his daughter. She was one fine-ass young girl, and instantly, my clitoris got warm and stiff in my underwear. My nipples began to get hard and all I could think about was getting her in the bed. I didn't want to dig a hole for myself, and I knew I needed to get the hell away from Fred, but with his daughter now coming into the picture, it would be hard.

The next day, I got a call from a very strange telephone number. I answered the call.

"Hello...hello?"

"Yes, may I speak with Envy please?" the sweet voice asked.

"This is she. Whom am I speaking with?" I asked.

"Oh, I'm so sorry. This is Dawn, Fred's daughter. How are you?"

"Oh okay, Dawn. Fred told me about you," I told her.

"I would like to meet with you tomorrow, if possible. Are there any entertainment shows or concerts happening in DC?" Dawn asked.

"Lauryn Hill is coming to town tomorrow night. Would you like to go see her at DAR Constitution Hall?" I responded with enthusiasm.

"Yes! I love Lauryn Hill."

"Okay, I'll buy the tickets first thing in the morning. I'll lock your number in my phone and call you after I get the tickets. We'll have lunch by noon," I told Dawn, while growing hornier for her young, sweet pussy.

*****

Early the next morning, I went to Ticketmaster and purchased two tickets for Lauryn Hill's concert. I met with Dawn about 12:30 p.m. at Bus Boys and Poet Eatery on 14th and U Street Northwest. I stood waiting in front of the restaurant until I saw Fred's pretty little girl.

"Hello, are you Dawn?" I asked the young lady, then looked at the picture Fred had sent to my cell phone to compare it to the person standing before me.

"Yes, that's me. You're Envy?"

"That's me," I said, and we laughed.

We ate and talked about many things. She told me that she was from Florida and going to move to Washington, DC. I told her that DC is a very nice city, especially the northeast part of town. Once we finished our lunch, I took her shopping at Tyson's Corner, spending about nine hundred dollars on her. Since she liked Gucci, I decided to buy her and myself an all Gucci outfit, including the shoes, to wear to the show.

After a few hours of hanging out, we went to my place to shower and change into our clothes. Then we headed to Constitution Hall. Nas had just hit the stage when we arrived. He came out rapping his song titled "Hate Me Now". He hit eight more of his songs, including "Ether", "One Mic" and Lauryn Hill came out and sung the hook to Nas' song "If I Ruled the World". He then left the stage.

Lauryn Hill's first song she sang was "Can't Take My Eyes Off Of You". Everyone stood up and sang along with the gorgeous black woman. She sung for about another hour and a half before belting out three of her hottest songs:

"Every Thing Is Everything", "To Zion" and "Ex Factor". Dawn got up out her seat and must have really been feeling "Ex Factor", because the young girl sang every lyric with emotion as if she were the one performing live in concert.

At the end of the show, Dawn expressed that she was tired and decided it would be best if I took her to my place. I smiled from ear to ear. I knew if Palm Beach Fred ever found out I was plotting to fuck his eighteen-year-old daughter, our friendship would never be the same.

When Dawn and I got to my place, I quickly went to my bedroom and grabbed something for Dawn to sleep in. Then I ran some bath water. Because we had a few drinks during intermission, I felt bold enough to walk up to Dawn and grab her around her waist.

"I can see in your eyes that you're curious about being with a woman, but you don't have to feel that way anymore. I want to show you how it feels to make love to another woman."

At first, Dawn looked surprised, but then, she grabbed my face with both hands and tongue kissed me. Before I could say anything, she took her clothes off. I did the same, and we jumped into the hot bubble bath that awaited us. We slowly kissed each other's lips and slid our tongues down each other's throats.

I looked at Dawn and said, "I'm a virgin; I've never had sex before."

"You're lying! Don't tell me that," Dawn responded, while I sucked on her grapefruit-size breasts. "Oh, that feels so good. I want my pussy sucked. Have you ever sucked pussy, Envy?" she asked as I stuck my finger in her hot pleasure hole.

Dawn moaned as I fulfilled her every sexual need. I enjoyed every moment as the seconds ticked away. As she finger-fucked herself in the ass, I sucked on her pussy, licking her clit with the tip of my tongue for damn near a half-hour until she splashed all over my mouth and face.

"You lied to me. How is it that you can make love to me like this and you're still a virgin?" she groaned.

The purpose of telling her that was so I could get Dawn to feel comfortable with the fact that I was a lot older than her and could definitely get the job done. We all have something that keeps our sexual partners coming back, and my tongue was the tool to get her sprung. With her having access to major cash, aka her dad Palm Beach Fred, I needed her to keep coming back, despite her being a little young for my liking.

To impress her, I called my dad and told him that I would have someone with me that night at Club Pure and needed her to see how important I am to some good fans of my film projects. Dad laughed, but he knew what time it was. So, he got a team of six females and six males ranging in age from eighteen to fifty.

When we stepped into Club Pure, located on 14th and U Streets Northwest, Dad's people played their parts to the fullest. As we walked further into the club, they approached me and asked for my autograph on huge posters, pictures, and even had small tablets for me to sign. Some asked me if I could take a picture with them. The set up for the long-range con was a success. Therefore, the griff could go on to phase three.

"Wow, I didn't know you are really like a superstar or something. Wait until I tell my dad. He's gonna be shocked," Dawn said with excitement, while looking into my eyes.

At that point, I knew I had the youngin' right where I wanted her.

Chapter 8
IMPATIENCE IS A CON MAN'S ENEMY

When we come in contact with most people, we always find ourselves trying to figure out what we can get from the other person. We try the old "put our cards on the table" trick, but most of the time, that doesn't work. Once you do that, you give the other person the upper hand, and they generally get what they want out of us.

Since I had the chance to work with a lot of doctors in the hospital, I got the opportunity to get to know some of them on a personal level. One doctor in particular was Dr. Downing. He was the type that liked to meet young women in the hospital, shower them with gifts, fuck them, and get them fired. He got away with it for years before I got there.

I watched his every move. His main weakness was young women ages eighteen to around twenty-three. In particular, he liked the ones who didn't have anything but the clothes on their backs and maybe a kid they were trying to raise with the help of their mother or grandmother, with the child's dad nowhere in sight.

When I figured out what he was doing, I felt the motherfucker needed to be taught a lesson. He got on my last nerve with the bullshit he did. I decided to hit him where it hurt - his motherfuckin' pocket!

Every chance I got, I went out of my way to speak to him. I wanted this fool not only to know my face, but to know me as a person, as well. In order to open the line of communication, I would often spark discussion with him about certain medicine and how it works in the body.

Dr. Downing boasted about being one of the greatest brain surgeons in the world. The government flew him all over the world to perform surgeries on people. He told me that he had been working at the hospital for more than twenty-five years.

"I've seen a lot of people come and go while working here," Dr. Downing said, pointing his finger at me.

I didn't like what he said. I knew exactly what he meant. It pissed me off, but in order to move forward with my plan, I had to keep my cool.

A few days later, Dr. Downing and I had lunch in the hospital's cafeteria. Since we had gotten cool, I figured it was time to put my plan in effect.

"Hello, Dr. Downing. How are you today?"

"I'm fine, Ms. Envy. I couldn't complain if I wanted to," Dr. Downing replied as he looked me up and down.

I could clearly see that he was sizing me up for the kill, just as he did many of his other young female victims.

That day, I wore this very short, very tight skirt suit to work that showed off my thick ass and huge cantaloupe-sized breasts. I made sure Dr. Downing saw me so I could put the thought of sex all in his head. This motherfucker started smiling from ear-to-ear when he saw how big my ass and breasts were.

"You're looking good in your sexy skirt. I didn't know you were so shapely," he commented.

"Well, Doctor, I guess I can say milk does the body good," I said, and we laughed.

I already set up a plan where I had my young female partner, Mia, ready to meet Dr. Downing. I told him about her and that she worked in the hospital as a volunteer. I also told him that she would be good for volunteer work in his office, as well. I explained to him that she was trying to get hired by the hospital in any position she could get. He said he would be interested in hiring some intern help and would like to meet with her. Dr. Downing gave me his office and cell numbers and told me to give them to Mia so he could set up an interview with her.

After lunch with Dr. Downing, I met with Mia and told her what she needed to do. A few days afterwards, Mia called Dr. Downing and set up a day and time to meet with him. A few weeks after their meeting, she was hired to work for him in his office. I told her to make sure she wore tight outfits that showed off her assets; eventually, he would bite the bait.

Mia was eighteen, but looked to be no older than fourteen. She could fool the best of people. Whenever we went out to a club, the guys working the door made sure to ask her for identification.

I constantly stayed in her ear every step of the way so she would follow all the rules of the game and not let impatience claim victory in this part of the con. Many con artists break the rule of patience; always be patient or you will fuck up your move before you have a chance to make it.

I told Mia to fuck the doctor as soon as she could. In addition, she was to make sure she got pictures of them fucking and some recorded conversations. Hell, I told her to get some video footage, if possible.

Mia went on to work for Dr. Downing at his office. Just like I figured, a few weeks down the line he started throwing sexual advances at her. One day, he offered to take Mia to dinner after work, and off to the races he went. She told me that he took her to one of the most expensive restaurants in Maryland. I believe Moe's Seafood Restaurant was the name of the place. She said they both ordered a stuffed lobster dinner with a baked potato and broccoli. Days later, she was still talking about the dinner they'd had.

"Girl, that food was so good. I told Dr. Downing that we could go there any time he wants to," Mia said.

"So what happened after y'all left the restaurant?" I asked.

"Envy girl, we went to the Days Inn in New Carrollton, and I fucked that old man until he began snoring so loud that the housekeeper knocked on the door and asked did we have any pets in our room," she told me, causing us both to laugh.

"I put my iPhone on the nightstand beside the bed, propped it up against the lamp, and recorded about an hour of the nastiest sex America could ever watch. First, I stroked his dick with my hand and got it hard as a rock. Then I put my wet lips on his thick, hard meat and gave him the best head of his life," Mia explained.

"Oh shit. What happened after that?"

"Then I put the dick in my creamy wet pussy and rode him like a true cowgirl," she said, laughing.

Mia went on to say they fucked two more times, and just as I asked her to do, she recorded it all on her iPhone.

As the weeks went by, I started getting in the motherfucker's pockets. Mia got the numbers, expiration date, and security numbers on the back of each and every one of his credit cards. I bought laptops, desktops, big-screen televisions, expensive clothes, and jewelry. I purchased everything I could before disposing of Dr. Downing's credit card numbers.

In the meantime, Mia found out Dr. Downing was married; she also found out his address where he and his wife lived. I must admit that she was doing a damn good job as a first-time grifter.

As Mia continued working for the sex fiend doctor, we dug deeper into his pockets before setting him up for the ultimate score. Figuring it was time to turn up the heat on Dr. Downing, I called Darlene, another one of my grifter friends, to help me take this sucker down. Darlene worked as a homicide detective for the metropolitan police department. I told her to act like she was Mia's mother and to go see Dr. Downing about him having sex with her underage daughter.

I filled Darlene in on the mark and what role she needed

to play on this fool. I made sure I would be in his office when Darlene showed up. As Dr. Downing, Mia, and I sat at a round table, we damn near jumped out our skin when we heard someone knock extremely hard. Mia got up and opened the door; it was Darlene.

"Mommy, I'm glad to see you. Did you come to take me home after work?" Mia asked, hugging Darlene at the door.

Ignoring Mia, Darlene walked through the door and into the office with her shiny metropolitan police badge in her left hand and her gun drawn in the other.

She pointed her gun straight at the doctor's head and screamed, "Are you the doctor that's fucking my fourteen-year-old daughter?"

Dr. Downing looked shocked and confused. "What are you talking about, ma'am? I don't know what you're talking about," the frightened doctor replied.

"That's my daughter right there, and she told me that she's been fucking you," Darlene said, pointing at Mia.

"I didn't know she was underage, officer. I'm an honest man and would not have had sex with her if I knew that," Dr. Downing said.

"Turn around and put your hands behind your back," Darlene ordered.

She walked up to the doctor and put handcuffs on his

wrists. The whole time, Dr. Downing pleaded with Darlene not to arrest him. I never saw a man so scared in my life.

"Detective, can I speak with the doctor for a moment before you take him to jail?" I asked Darlene, who had started talking on her walkie-talkie.

"Yeah, you can talk to him for a moment," Darlene replied.

I stood and approached Dr. Downing to whisper in his ear. I told him that he should offer the detective a large sum of money and maybe the situation would go away. He looked as if a light bulb clicked on in his head.

"Yes, that's a good idea. *You* make her an offer and I'll pay it. Let her know I will pay her and Mia to just make this mistake go away. Please, please, talk to them for me, Envy. Hell, I'll pay you, too, if you can make it happen," Dr. Downing voiced with a worry-filled tone.

"I got this, Doctor. Just leave it up to me. I'm gonna make this go away," I told him, then turned my attention to Darlene. "Detective, may I talk with you in another room, please?"

After Darlene and I stepped into another room, I told her to raise her voice and act as if she really wanted to kill the doctor.

"I want to shoot that motherfucker in his fucking head for

having sex with my teenaged daughter! That son of a bitch!" she yelled.

I winked to let her know she was doing a great job.

"Calm down, Detective, just calm down. Dr. Downing wants to settle this matter."

"Settle it how?" Darlene yelled loud enough for him to hear. "The only way he can settle this is by going to jail for the next fifteen years. That's how I think he can settle this!"

"No, Detective, please listen for a moment," I said in a slightly raised voice so I could be sure the doctor heard me trying to fight for his freedom. "He wants to settle this in a way where you won't feel bad about the agreement."

"Okay, and exactly what way is that?" Darlene asked.

"Dr. Downing will agree to pay you one hundred thousand dollars to make this situation disappear," I said loudly.

I knew he'd pay just about any amount of cash to avoid going to jail and losing his license to practice medicine.

"If he's willing to get me one hundred thousand dollars cash money from the bank right fucking now, I'll let him go! And that's the only way!" Darlene yelled.

I went into the other room where Dr. Downing was sitting and asked him if he could get a hundred thousand dollars right now.

"Yes, I can get the money with no problem," he replied, looking at me with a look of relief and gratitude.

Darlene followed the doctor to the bank in an unmarked police car. After collecting the hundred thousand dollars from Dr. Downing, she met us at a nearby hotel in Largo, Maryland right off of Landover Road. The three of us split the money three ways and celebrated with a toast for knocking the mark off for a nice piece of cash.

Chapter 9

I WANT TO HAVE SOME CRAZY SEX

One morning, I woke up about two o'clock after experiencing the wildest dream of my life. In the dream, I was a captain in the U.S. Army, and we were at battle with another country. The funny thing about it was we were fighting an all-woman army. Two different countries fighting and both Armed Forces were comprised totally of women.

There were all types of guns, bombs, tanks, and weapons. We were killing a lot of them, and they were killing a lot of us. The real trip was they were all black American women and we were, too. It was taking place in the middle of the District of Columbia, more like the southeast part of the city. Black smoke filled the air from burning vacant buildings, just like in the war movies.

James Tanner

My troops and I made our way through the South Capitol section of Southeast, where we got into a shootout with other enemy troops. It was a shootout like I had never seen. Troops fell dead on both sides of the street as I fired my M-16 semi-automatic weapon. Taking aim at a crowd of twenty combat women, I killed seventeen of them. We captured a captain and two of her soldiers as my troops and I crept up on them from the side of a burning apartment building.

"Alright, you bitches, drop your weapons and put your hands up in the air before I start blasting you hoes," I said, my troops and me rolling up on them bitches and catching them by surprise.

After grabbing the guns off the ground, we took the bitches into custody. We walked behind the female soldiers for about three miles before reaching a concentration camp for our prisoners of war. I made all them bitches take a hot shower while I watched their fine asses shake like Jell-O. When they raised their legs to wash between their soft, round ass cheeks, my mouth got watery, and my pussy began to get wet for some tongue action and a hard, strap-on dildo.

I made the female captain come to my office and fuck me with her long tongue like a horny dyke in a federal penitentiary. This woman had one great body on her. Her measurements were 38-24-45, her curves in all the right places. I couldn't keep my eyes off of this hoe. She was one bad bitch. The captain came in my office and wasted no time putting my pussy straight in her mouth, as if she knew what I wanted off the top. She slowly licked and sucked my clit before tongue fucking my asshole. I laid my head back and opened my legs wide. It felt so good that I grabbed the bitch's head and tried to put it inside my pussy. After cumming in the captain's mouth, I wanted more, ready for a second round. So, I grabbed my adult toy bag, handed her my thirteen-inch strap-on dildo, and made her fuck me from behind.

"Oh shit! Fuck me, Captain, with your long, hard dick, baby. Fuck me until I hurt. That dick is so damn big," I yelled with intense sexual contentment.

She fucked me every way we could think of with that big, plastic dick. With plenty of baby oil and her stamina together, all I could do was cum again and again. I came so much that I almost passed the fuck out. Still, I wanted more with this hoe.

Like a thirsty cat licking from a bowl of milk, I sucked on her pussy. The bitch went wild when I started to slowly lick her asshole. I stuck my finger in and out of her pussy every time I licked or sucked her pretty, round asshole. She moaned louder each time I tongue fucked her. I grabbed the long, thick dildo, strapped it on, and fucked her. The dick was a bit too large for the woman, but she took it like a real soldier.

She had a tiny little pussy, but the dick must have felt good to her because she took every inch. I fucked that woman for about two hours, while she yelled, "Ouch...ooh....ouch. I love this dick. It hurts, but I love pain. Hurt my pussy, baby!"

I told her to get on her knees. When she did, I stood up, and she put the big, plastic dick in her mouth. She sucked it like a champion dick sucker. Deep throat would be an understatement for what she was doing.

After fucking her mouth with the dildo, I put a condom on the barrel of my M-16 semi-automatic rifle, then told her to get on all fours and open her ass cheeks. I fucked her in the ass with the long barrel of my gun until the bitch had an orgasm. After I pulled the barrel out her ass, I woke up.

I wasn't mad at her, though. I wet my sheets up with a good nut, and I was quite sure the captain in my dream wasn't mad either.

If you'd like to have some crazy sex like that, just close your eyes and think about what I just told you about this chick. Then rub your clit until you cum. The mind is a powerful thing...and very stimulating, as well.

Chapter 10
WOW!

In order to draw your victims to you, you must be kind and treat them in a caring manner. Never look sloppy as far as being drunk on alcohol, high on any illegal drugs, or dirty and smelly. Your clothes and shoes have to be fresh, and your body must be clean. If not, this will make your mark have a lack of trust for you. That means you will blow the frame before you can get it started. My dad always told me how important it is to misdirect your mark with a visual of a clean image.

I gathered up a few of my female comrades, and it was time to go to work. One of the biggest male rappers in the world had a birthday party at DC's most famous nightclub,

Love. Television news cameras were set up right in front of the club as Lyin' Lyn, Juicy, and I stood in line to get into the party. Thirty minutes passed as we stood in the long line.

A black stretch limousine pulled up and sat for ten minutes before one of the biggest rappers of the universe got out and screamed out, "It's time to throw down DC! This is yo' boy Big Romeo and I'm here to celebrate my birthday! Y'all ready to party?"

He smiled and pointed at the crowd as he walked from the limousine and into the club.

After an hour or so, the girls and I finally made it inside the club. We headed straight for the VIP section on the third floor. We had to make our move on Big Romeo as soon as possible. All stupid-ass men fall for a bitch with a big ass, big breasts, and who says she's ready to suck some dick. The girls and I were wearing our tight skirts, push-up bras, and had a hoochie look on our faces as if we were ready to go to the hotel. Big Romeo bit our bait. He had one of his men come get us and bring us to his section in the VIP area.

"I want you and your crew to hang out with us after the club," Big Romeo whispered in my ear.

"Okay," I replied. "That's fine, but where are we going?"

Big Romeo pulled out a large stack of one-hundred-dollar bills and said, "I have a lot of money, and I want to spend it on you and your girlfriends. Does it matter?"

Stuck, I was at a loss for words for a second. I didn't want to blow our frame and lose the opportunity to take this mark for his cash, so I had to play it smooth and let him think he had the power.

We partied with him and his crew, but when Big Romeo and his crew went on stage, I took that opportunity to tell the girls what to do once we got to the hotel with him after the show.

For about an hour and a half, Big Romeo and his entourage worked the stage as he rapped four of his number one hits: "Girls Fuck Girls Better", "Let Me See You Eat Her, Boo", "Big Booty Girls" and "Do You Want Your Ass Licked". The crowd went wild, and the women were trying to grab him as he walked from one side of the stage to the other.

I told the girls that whomever Big Romeo wanted between us, that particular person would act as if she liked her clothes ripped off like she was being raped. One of us would record it on our cell phone, save the footage, and call the hotel security before it went any further.

I waited until Big Romeo got off stage, then walked over to him and whispered in his ear, "Hey, my girl Juicy wants to fuck. She gets really horny when a man snatches her clothes off and rips her underwear, almost as if she's role playing about being raped."

Big Romeo smiled. "Oh yeah? That's what she likes?"

"Yes. She's a cold freak, boo. She also said she thinks you have a little dick," I said, playing him against his ego.

I knew Big Romeo felt he had something to prove, and that was just what I wanted him to think.

The girls and I rode to the hotel with Big Romeo, while his entourage rode in a separate limousine. We talked and shared a lot of laughs during our ride, but the second we got in the hotel room, Big Romeo ripped off Juicy's skirt and blouse. Lyin' Lyn recorded the whole situation on her camera phone.

They had plenty to drink in the hotel room, but I told the girls not to drink any alcohol. We had to keep our minds on the money and let their minds be on the pussy. As time went on, his boys got drunk. That's when shit got out of hand.

The dudes took the camera phone with the footage and broke the phone. Then they ripped our clothes off and raped the three of us. They threatened to pay someone to find and kill us if we told anyone.

I'm not going to lie; I was scared than a motherfucker. I never experienced anything like that before. It was fucked up, but it was a risk we took. My girls and I were beaten and raped; afterwards, my pussy was hurting more than it ever had. It seemed like some shit that happened in that movie *Player's Club*.

The funny thing about it, we were not prepared for shit like that. I never saw it coming, but it was part of the game. Win some, lose some. It's all about the investigation on the mark, what's already known, what needs to be known, and all the risks.

After Big Romeo and his boys fucked us for hours, one after another, they finally left the hotel room. It must have been about nine o'clock the next morning, nearly eight hours later.

As the girls and I started to leave, I spotted the cell phone with the recorded footage of the rape over on the corner. I got the chip out of the broken phone and took it to hotel security, who called the police. A few days later, the cops went to the famous rapper's home to arrest him and his boys on rape charges.

We didn't get any money out that deal, but I sure learned a very important lesson. Always remember to never be in a situation you can't control. It was certainly one rule I would never break again.

Chapter 11

WORK HARD, BUT PLAY HARDER

The girls and I finally got over the shit that happened to us at the hotel with Big Romeo and his boys. Even though they were all arrested, we still decided to get even with them fools, but at a later time. As a matter of fact, a spokesperson from Big Romeo's record label offered us thirty thousand dollars not to show up in court, and that's what we did. We got ten thousand dollars each, so we chalked it up as a done deal and charged the rest of the shit to the game. I still plan to get even with them dudes, but at a different time and another day.

After making that money, I decided to go on a vacation and relax a little while. I went to San Francisco to chill. During my travels, I met some very interesting people. I met a lesbian author named CoCo Sweets, who wrote a few urban street novels. She was a pretty brown-skinned female who had a very nice shape. She stood about five-foot-six and weighed approximately one hundred and thirty-five pounds. This bitch was one fine-ass woman, and I had to have her.

I went into the Alexander Bookstore between Market and Mission Street and saw she was having a book signing. It was a long line of people standing with her books in their hands, waiting for their turn to get them signed by her. Like everyone else, I stood in line, as well. When it was finally my turn to get my book signed, she held out her hand to shake mine.

"Hello, CoCo. My name is Envy. I heard so much about your book that I had to purchase it," I told her.

"Great! I'm glad to hear that. Do you know how hard I work to keep my fans satisfied with my writing? Thank you so much, Envy."

"Sure, no problem. I'm a filmmaker, and I know how hard it is to make your projects the best," I replied.

CoCo stopped autographing my book and looked up at me. "If you're a filmmaker, you're just the one I need to speak with."

"Okay, that's cool. We need to exchange phone numbers and talk later, if that's good with you."

CoCo agreed and we exchanged telephone numbers.

I didn't want to look at her as a mark, and I really didn't want to run any con on her. However, since I was an opportunist, if she gave me the opportunity, I would get her. Even though I sold her a lie when I told her that I was a filmmaker, my motive wasn't to get her money; it was to get her.

I called CoCo about a week later to set up a day and time for us to meet and have lunch. After a couple minutes of standing in front of the Lu Lu Restaurant and Bar at 816 Folsom Street in San Francisco, I saw a candy apple red 500E Mercedes Benz pull up. CoCo waved to me.

"Hey, Envy! I'm trying to park. Go in and get our seats. I'll be right in," CoCo yelled out the window.

Going inside, I got seated and waited for her to join me. She walked in the door and over to our table. We talked about some of her novels and why she started writing books. I figured I'd keep the ball in her lap and let her keep talking about herself. That way, I could learn things about her, such as what she liked and what she didn't like. Knowing such things would help me in doing all the right things to stay on her good side and in the frame. For those who don't know, stay in the frame means to stay in the picture.

She shared a lot of things about herself, and it seemed I had met her at the right time. She was a single woman who had been abused by men all her life, and she was bitter about her mother and father being crack addicts. Although she was college educated, I clearly saw that her life was far from an easy one.

My father, Ace Spinner, always told me that power comes in numbers and to always have people in my circle that could look the part of what I may need to pull a big con off. It was important for them to have a good reputation and the credibility of some sort of professional.

After that day, CoCo and I started hanging out constantly. We went to clubs, parties, stage plays, and even concerts.

After six months, we were in an intimate relationship. CoCo liked me to show her just how special she was to me. So, I made sure that every week on Friday, I had flowers for her when I came home, even though I traveled back and forth to San Francisco from Washington, DC. I went to book signings with her and traveled to many of the book expos as well as the literary book conferences. It was nothing like seeing my woman doing it big as she promoted her book.

I was that partner to her that most people search an entire lifetime to find. In order to have someone in a way that they have never been had before, you have to do things for them that no one has ever done. In this day and age, there are not many people in this world made of real substance. It's only a hand full of them in every ten thousand people that really have values to the degree of worth. I didn't make my dollars honestly, but when it came down to being a team player and a woman with values, that's me all the motherfuckin' way.

Believe me, I loved what I did for a living, and I loved the excitement of the fact that I might not have gotten away with my next con. There was always the possibility that I might go to jail or lose my life. Who knows? However, being a con man or woman was like the fuckin' National Basketball Association. You got to love this game!

CoCo and I traveled around the world promoting her book so much that I began to learn a lot about the book publishing game. I promised myself that I would write a book for the world to learn from; I was that bitch that the school system should create a college course about. If you or anyone you know chooses to ever listen to me or do the things I did, you'll always make a bank roll. Follow my lead, and all bitches will eat! So, when my first book comes out, just make sure you purchase it if you want to know some real game to keep your pockets pumped up. Your money will begin to rise, and your game will be on one thousand.

CoCo had a book signing at the Book Expo of America in New York City. As she sat at a table near the publishing company Harper Collins, she had a long line of people waiting for her to sign their books.

"Envy, over here, honey!" CoCo yelled to me as she waved her hand for me to help out at the table. "Baby, can you hand out flyers to my fans as I sign the books for them?" she asked.

"Sure, honey, no problem," I said.

While she continued to sign books, I handed out flyers promoting her next book. Even though I wasn't used to doing this type of shit, it was all about her and her movement.

CoCo sold about four hundred of her books for fifteen dollars apiece. The money inspired me and gave me a reason to make her cum when we got back to the hotel.

Once in our hotel room, we showered, and immediately afterwards, I sucked her pussy, wanting to taste her milky, sweet cum in my mouth like a fat kid wanting cake and ice cream. A woman's clitoris has about eight thousand nerves, so I knew to start right there with her thick, swollen clit right on my tongue. CoCo opened her legs, holding them wide and up in the air, as I tongued her down.

"Oh shit, baby. Oh my, your tongue is on one hundred. You need to put that head in a can and sell it by the six-pack,"

CoCo moaned as I stuck my middle finger in her asshole.

I sucked her pussy and finger-fucked her straight in the ass until she skeeted her juices damn near across the room.

"Bitch, you made me have a real orgasm. Did you see my cum shoot out my pussy? It must have gone at least three feet across the room," CoCo said.

My pussy was soaking wet just seeing CoCo enjoying the long, breathtaking, oral sex I gave her. After busting her nuts, she turned me on my stomach, grabbed the twelve-inch dildo, and strapped it on her. She then proceeded to fuck me hard from the back until my pussy ached. I didn't complain, though; I sometimes liked to feel the aching pain from my pussy. It let me know I had been fucked hard and good.

As I lay in bed after climaxing, my cell phone rang. It was Palm Beach Fred. I wondered how long it would be before he called me again.

"Hello, Fred? How are you doing? It's been a while since we talked," I answered, playing it off like I had been looking forward to his call.

"I'm fine, my queen. I just want to thank you for taking care of my daughter when she came in town."

"No problem, Fred. Anything for you," I said, while hoping he had not found out that I was fucking his sexy-ass daughter.

"I need to see you soon, Envy. I have some investors who are looking for a project to invest their money into. I know you have something going on or someone in your clique needs some investors, so I want you to make me look good by having your people to help my people," he told me.

Instantly, I started thinking about what kind of con I could put together. I didn't want to bring CoCo Sweets in the game because she was a square, and one of the rules of the con game is never cheat a friend, but never give a sucker an even chance. I told Fred that I needed a few days to think about it and that I would get back to him as soon as possible.

Chapter 12

THE THINGS PEOPLE DO FOR MONEY ARE THE SAME THINGS THEY DO FOR FREE

Dad always said a kid must have a good support system from home to help elevate the talent he or she possesses within. On many occasions, we see kids or teenagers who possess talent, but because they don't have their family's support or a family with the money needed to get in the right places the world never gets the opportunity to see their skills.

I was sitting outside at a café, when I noticed a woman walking by that looked like someone I grew up with.

"Jean? Mean Jean?" I called out as the woman slowly walked past the table.

"Hello. Do I know you from somewhere?" she asked.

I replied, "Yes, we went to school together. You use to run track, right?"

"Yes, I did. You remember that?" the woman responded loudly.

"You use to run so fast in high school that everyone called you Mean Jean because you were mean with it when you would compete against other track teams," I said as she looked around.

I noticed that Mean Jean's clothes were dirty, and she had a very bad odor coming from her body.

"Is everything okay with you?" I asked the very slender ex-track champion.

Mean Jean looked at me with a very strange expression on her face before she answered. A teardrop rolled down her face from her left eye.

"Things have been very bad for me ever since I left DC. Drug dealers gunned down my parents and baby brother. I jumped out the window and ran for my life."

"So how did you end up here in San Francisco?" I asked.

"First, let me ask you your name. So much has happened in my life that I can't remember anything," Mean Jean said.

"I'm Envy."

"Oh yeah, I remember you. You were very well known in high school back in the day. You had everybody wanting you or wanting to be like you, even me. Yes, I was into girls back then, and I still like women today," Jean shared.

"So, Jean, I want you to finish the story. What happened after you realized your family had been killed?" I asked inquisitively.

"I didn't know what else to do but to leave DC. I knew I was a gay woman; therefore, I needed to be somewhere where I could feel comfortable. I heard so much about San Francisco, and that's why I'm here," she said.

Mean Jean told me that the murders had never been solved and she knew for sure the drug dealers that killed her family would eventually come and murder her, as well. She also told me that she had stolen the money and drugs the dealers were looking for when they came to her parents' apartment. She said she snorted cocaine for a short period of time before someone showed her how to turn the powder cocaine into a crack rock form. At the time, she didn't know how much she stole. However, she knew it was a lot of cocaine and a large duffel bag full of money, and because of that, her family lost their lives.

"So you never came clean about your stealing money and drugs?" I asked.

James Tanner

"No, I never told the police, if that's what you're asking me."

"Damn. So, you're the real reason why your family was killed?" I asked Jean straight out.

"Yes. If it weren't for me stealing the drugs and the money, my family would still be alive today. I hurt deeply every day. I started using cocaine, and now I've been homeless and smoking crack for the last eleven years," she said.

"So where do you stay?' I inquired.

"I stay at a homeless shelter right down the street. That's where I was on my way to," Jean said.

I handed her one of business cards that had my cell number on it and told her to call me. Then she walked off.

After I finished eating, I called CoCo to see where she was so we could meet up and plan her book signing tour. CoCo's cell phone rang about five times before she answered.

"Hey, sweetheart, this is your other half. What are you doing?" I said softly into the phone.

"I'm at the library talking with the supervisor of the staff. What's going on?" CoCo responded quietly.

"Everything is fine. I was trying to figure out what bookstores you want to do your book signings at?"

"Well, I think I'll start with Barnes and Noble. We will set up a fifteen-store book tour with them, and from there, we will do the same with Books A Million."

CoCo gave me a list of numbers to the Barnes and Noble stores in that area, and I made calls to each and every one of them. I didn't have a problem with doing any assistant work for CoCo, because I had decided that I would write my very own book some day, and I planned to have my very own publishing company, also. I would have a list of authors under contract at my publishing company, too. So, whatever she needed me to do, I was down for it. Therefore, I made call after call to all the Barnes and Noble bookstores in the local area.

By the time I finished, our schedule was full for the next six weeks. I really enjoyed setting up the signings, because it seemed like a vacation to me whenever we were traveling. I didn't have to run con on anyone, although I set up a few marks for some game at a later date. Other than that, it was a chance for me to learn new things and relax at the same time.

Even though I was working hard with assisting CoCo with her book signing tour, I still kept in close contact with Mean Jean. I knew that she knew the low down on what went on in San Francisco, and I needed her to tell me everything she knew.

CoCo was on a roll with the signings. After we finished the six-week book signing tour with Barnes and Noble Bookstores, we started with Books A Million. We did book signings in twelve stores over the course of twelve days. By the time we were finished, I was tired as hell, but it was well worth the time and the hard work.

Three days later, I got a call from Mean Jean. I talked to her for about an hour before deciding to meet up with her at a nearby McDonald's later that evening. When I caught up with Mean Jean, she told me about this dealer that she purchased her cocaine from. She called her Marlene 'The Cocaine Queen'. Mean Jean told me that Marlene sold a lot of drugs and that she was a very smart, beautiful woman. Curious, I asked if Marlene was a lesbian.

"I'm not sure if she is or not. One minute, she's chillin' with a bunch of females, but later, I'll see her with a bunch of men. The men who she hangs out with are men that sell a bunch of drugs," Jean said. "But, the females who she hangs out with sell dope, too. So, it's pretty hard to figure her out."

"Have you ever seen any of the dudes who come to see her treat her special, like they're fucking?" I asked.

Jean bit into her Big Mac. "No, not really. They just come by her place pushing expensive cars and designer clothes. I have seen them bring her expensive champagne, but that's about the extent of it to my knowledge," Jean said, wiping her mouth with a napkin. "I want to get off this shit," she continued. "I need to be drug free and living a good life like everyone else. I have dreams of still being successful," Jean said as a tear rolled down her cheek.

"Yes, I agree. If you're ready to stop smoking crack, I'm willing to help you. We can find a drug rehab program for you to go to ASAP." I hugged Mean Jean and was ready to take on the challenge of helping her get clean.

We finished eating, and I took Jean with me to do some shopping. I picked up a few outfits for CoCo, and I purchased a few outfits for Mean Jean, also.

Later that night, I took the special gifts that I purchased for CoCo home so I could make her smile. I knew she had been working hard with her book signings, and now I wanted to put some work in, but not in a literary way. I had an overwhelming urge to eat her pussy until the sun came up.

"Hey, sweetheart, I have something for you. Here, take these bags, baby," I said, handing the two large bags to her.

"What did you get me? I figured you would come in the house with some gifts for me. You know I love gifts," CoCo said, then kissed me in the mouth.

I grabbed her pretty, round ass cheeks and straight tongued her down. Then I took her by the hand and headed to the bathroom, where I ran a bubble bath for us to relax and get clean in the process to prepare for our all-night sexual adventure.

I lit the five candles that surrounded the bathtub before starting to wash CoCo's pretty brown-skinned body. I started with her sexy breasts. As I washed her pretty brown titties, I slowly licked her nipples until they got so hard that they pointed outward. CoCo lay back in the tub. I ducked my head underwater and licked her wet, hard clitoris. I sucked and licked her pussy while going back and forth under the water, only coming up for air. Whenever I did come up for air, I sucked on her neck, breasts, and shoulders to keep her sexually stimulated.

When I finally got my breathing back to normal, I took CoCo to the bedroom, strapped on my thick, long dildo, and fucked her hard until she came uncontrollably. I fucked her so good that she fell straight the fuck out with cum still running out her tender, swollen pussy lips. After I put her to sleep, I called it a night my damn self.

Chapter 13

MANY ARE CALLED, BUT FEW ARE CHOSEN

We all were put on this earth for something. Every day that goes by, there is a reason why you lived that day out to see the next one. Whatever it is you're good at must be pursued, because you only get one shot at it.

Mean Jean checked into a drug rehabilitation program. The past five weeks had been a very hard task for me insofar as sticking by CoCo Sweets and standing by my word to help her get clean. Even though I kept in mind that I must use everyone for personal gain, I had a heart sometimes. I hustled blessings, too. I felt that one day, I might find myself in a situation where a blessing may be the only thing that can save my ass. Remember, not everything can be for monetary gain.

I had absolutely no contact with Mean Jean during her time in detoxification, so I wanted to know how she was doing or if she needed anything.

My cell phone rang about six times before I answered.

"Hello?"

"Hello, Envy. This is Jean. How's it going out there?"

"Hey, Jean. What's going on? Can I bring you anything? I know you could use a few things," I said.

"Yes, that's why I'm calling. I'm going to be released on Monday. So, I wanted to know if you could come get me?"

"Yes, I can come get you, Jean. What kind of question is that? I told you once and I'll tell you again. I'm with you all the way."

In the background, I could hear one of the counselors telling Mean Jean it was her time to get off the phone. So, we ended the call.

I asked CoCo if Mean Jean could live with us for a while until she got her life in some kind of order.

"I don't like the idea of Jean living with us, but since you're trying to help her, I'll respect your decision, if that's what you want to do. I don't like dealing with people who don't have their lives straight, because I had bad experiences while trying to help so-called friends," she expressed.

"Don't worry about anything, baby. I have everything covered."

I never trusted too many people; the people we often trust are sometimes the first to leave you hanging. Letting my guard down was not an option. I made the exception for Mean Jean, though, because she could be used for a great purpose for my hustle – when the time was right.

Monday rolled around, and I went to the drug rehab to pick up Jean. She had gained weight and her skin cleared up so good that she began to look attractive to me. Her breast size blew up to a 46D-cup and her ass blew out to forty-six inches, but she still had a small twenty-four waist. I asked Mean Jean what she wanted to do since she was back out in the street now.

"The first thing I want to do is get something to eat," she said as I stopped at the red traffic light.

We decided to go to a seafood restaurant called Fisherman's Wharf. I ordered the Ultimate Seafood Platter and Mean Jean ordered The Fisherman's Platter. I had lobster, crab legs, shrimp, crab cakes, and a lot other shit that I couldn't eat because the plate was full of so much seafood. Jean's plate was full of seafood, too, but not as much as mine.

As we sat and ate together, I had the chance to tell her a little bit about CoCo. I told Jean that CoCo really didn't like the idea of her staying with us, but she approved her stay because I wanted to help an old high school friend.

"CoCo is a real sweet woman, and I respect her. I've learned a lot from her, and I look forward to writing my own book soon because of her."

My advice to Mean Jean? "Stay focused on what you need, and stay far out of her way until y'all bond. When y'all become friends, things will work out just fine."

Chapter 14

SEX, TOYS, AND THE THREE OF US

CoCo started to open up. I was glad to see the change in her. I understood she had it rough where she grew up; therefore, her trust for people was next to none. She told me how her own mother didn't like her, and she had never met her father. All the girls in the neighborhood picked fights with her because she was pretty and had all the young boys chasing after her in junior high and high school. Even though she fought back, it was some shit she felt she had no control over, and no one was there to protect her.

I totally understood because it was a lot of shit that I could identify with, and that was no bullshit. Even though CoCo was a very sweet, young woman, she could be cold as a block of ice to anyone if she felt disrespected. She could

James Tanner

change up on a person in a split second. The only way I could deal with her during those times was to remember all of the shit in her life that I came behind.

When in relationships, we have to understand how the other person in the relationship was brought up and understand that out of all the good and bad shit this person has been through mentally, it could be a lot going on in that person's head that we may never understand or adapt to. Also, we need to keep in mind that some of these so-called parents raised their children in a fucked-up manner, and we are coming behind all of that shit. If a parent drinks alcohol and fights all day, their kids will most likely grow up and do the same shit because that's the way he or she was raised.

Always pay close attention to what you are coming behind when dealing with a person. Most of the time we have to know these things so we will know how to deal with different types of people. If your friend or special someone lies to you all the time, then you know this person is living in an illusive world and is sick mentally. Quickly, you must try to understand what are you identifying with, because something is making you stick around. Also, understand that you can never trust anyone that tells you a lie. They can never be trusted, and if they lie to you, it simply lets you know that person is not your friend.

Never be afraid to question yourself in any situation. It will make you take a second look, and at that point, you may get the answer you're looking for, if you're smart enough to pinpoint it.

Mean Jean and I talked about her future plans.

"Well, Envy, I'm going to apply for some jobs and all that square shit, but I'm a bitch from the street. Any way I can make something happen, I'm down for it," Mean Jean said.

That's what I was waiting to hear. She was definitely talking my kind of talk. All I needed to do was get in her head to find out what she knew.

"Okay, that's what's up. We can make some moves for sure, but I just need to know what we can make a move on," I said, while looking into her beautiful brown eyes.

"Well, the broad that I talked to you about before I went into the program named Marlene would be a first to start with. We must use finesse, because she has a crew that is extremely dangerous. She sells a lot of cocaine, but that bitch is dangerous," Mean Jean softly stated.

"A'ight, we can set up a plan to get money out that bitch later. We should move on Treasure Trove Jewelry Store…"

*****

One week later, we made our move.

Two days before we put the plan in action, we went to a nearby costume store that sold everything to help someone disguise themselves as a police officer. I purchased a badge, uniform, bulletproof vest, gun with a holster, and a pair of handcuffs. We got everything fitted just right, and by the time we finished, she had the look of a real police officer.

A few days later, it was time to execute our move. I walked into the jewelry store and looked at some pieces of jewelry, mainly diamond rings and diamond bracelets. I called the saleswoman over to me and showed her an estate of jewelry that I wanted to see. I pointed out to her a matching ring, necklace, and earrings set. She pulled it from the glass display case and told me the sale price was forty thousand dollars. I told her that I had forty thousand in cash and wanted to purchase the estate. Then I counted out forty thousand dollars in counterfeit bills on the counter.

About five minutes into our transaction, Mean Jean walked into the jewelry store, flashed her police badge in the young saleswoman's face, and said, "Ma'am, please back up. These bills are counterfeit, and I must confiscate these bills and the jewelry as evidence. We have been following this woman during our investigation."

Mean Jean put the jewelry in clear plastic crime bags and

told the woman that a police investigation team would be coming to visit her in a few days. She then grabbed me by the arm and walked me out of the store. Once we got out the jewelry store, we ran two blocks away, jumped into my car, and pulled off. We had just worked the bitch out of forty thousand dollars' worth of jewelry.

I was on such a high that I felt the need to go home and have a threesome with CoCo and Mean Jean.

"I'm one horny bitch when I get money in my pockets. The best way to get to my heart is through my pockets, not my pussy," I said as we drove through a green light.

Later that night, Mean Jean and I went to the house. CoCo had just finished taking a shower. It was the right time to get my fuck on. I went into the bedroom and sat down in the chair next to our king-sized bed.

"Come over here and put that pretty pink pussy of yours in my face."

CoCo took off her bathrobe and walked over to me. She stood up in the chair and opened her legs so I could lick her pussy. She humped my mouth, coming all over my hot, juicy tongue. When I noticed Mean Jean in the doorway of my bedroom, I winked at her and motioned her with my finger to join CoCo and me in our hot, passionate, lovemaking session.

Mean Jean came into the room and started licking CoCo's

James Tanner

ass. I picked CoCo up and put her on the bed. As I moved, Mean Jean opened her ass cheeks, and I licked the crack of her ass. I removed my clothes off so I could fuck both of them the way they needed to be fucked. Grabbing my fourteen-inch dildo, I strapped it on. Since Mean Jean was licking CoCo's asshole from the doggy style position, I pulled her jeans and underwear down and started fucking her with my hard dick from the back. Mean Jean collapsed with twenty-five hard, quick strokes of the dick. It was obvious the dick was too damn big for her.

I had to realize that most women couldn't take a fourteen-inch *real* dick, so I knew she probably couldn't take a fourteen-inch dildo. In order for us to continue, I had to take that big motherfucker out of Mean Jean's tight pussy. She held her stomach for a few seconds, but then jumped right back into the action. I wanted to make sure Mean Jean got her thing off, as well. I told Mean Jean to suck my dick while I ate CoCo's pussy.

I lay back on the bed with my hard dildo sticking straight up in the air. Before Mean Jean started to suck it, CoCo rode the long, thick dick and had another orgasm. A thick, white, milky cream ran down the sides of the dildo as her eyes rolled back in her head and closed. She held her stomach and shook like she was going into an epileptic convulsion. It scared me

124

for a minute, but I realized again that it was the big black dick meat that shut them all down.

Mean Jean sucked on the dick. I watched her give me the best slow neck she could ever give. As she continued to suck up, down, and around the head of the rubber dick, I enjoyed hearing the sucking sounds that came from her lips. I enjoyed it so much, it made me cum. Mean Jean's jaws began to hurt from her mouth being open so wide. Since I had already came, I told her to just relax while I went into the bathroom and took a long hot shower.

When I finished, I told Mean Jean where the towels and washcloths were so she could clean herself up, as well. Then I got in the bed, curled up behind CoCo, and went straight to sleep.

*****

The next morning, I reserved a roundtrip plane ticket to Washington, DC so I could get rid of the jewelry. I called Dad and told him to set up a meeting with his people in Georgetown where we normally sold jewels after stealing them. He was in the process of working a mark himself, but he was on point and would be ready when I got back to DC.

The next day, I told CoCo and Mean Jean that I had an

emergency and had to fly back to Washington, DC.

I winked my eye at Mean Jean and whispered, "I'll have some money for you when I get back." I told CoCo that I would have something special for her, as well.

My flight was at two o'clock that afternoon, so we had lunch at the airport. I boarded the plane shortly after that. It really didn't take long to get back to DC from San Francisco because I slept the whole flight.

Chapter 15
SCAMS, SCOUNDELS, AND SUCKERS

Dad always told me to never love anyone. When you have someone in love with you, you can squeeze them like a lemon. When you don't have any love, you can control your feelings and nothing they do can hurt you. It's about doing all the things that a person would do when they're in love, but it's all an act. You're on stage. Once you see how they want to be treated and know what they like, then you can control them all the way to their bank account. When you think about the years or months you spent around them, always remember that it's all a hustle if you feel your heart getting involved. Practice on everybody, because practice make perfect. That's a rule Dad said to never break.

Dad waited outside in a limousine at Ronald Reagan Airport as soon as my flight touched down around 5:15 p.m. I walked out the front door and there stood my father.

"Hey, Daddy," I yelled out, running to his open arms.

"Hey, my little angel," he said, hugging me and giving me a kiss on the side of my face.

As I got into the limousine, I saw his two partners, Kid Twist and Suitcase Murphy, sitting there with a bottle of White Star Moet.

"So what are we celebrating?" I asked, while Dad poured the champagne in a tall glass.

"We're celebrating the presence of you, my dear. It has been a long time since I had the chance to hang out with my daughter. I love you so much, sweetheart."

When Dad said that to me, I could have melted like chocolate. There's nothing like a dad's love for his daughter.

I pulled the jewelry from my purse and showed my father and his two partners.

"Damn, that's some nice shit there, girl!" Suitcase Murphy said, while I held the earrings, necklace, and ring in the air.

"Yeah, that's nice. You really came off with that move," Kid Twist stated as I handed the jewels over to him.

"I taught you very well, sweetheart. Ever since you were a

little girl, I saw the need to teach you the game, baby. Now, as long as you keep your heart out the game, you'll be fine. Love is for suckers, and many of them are born every day. We can go straight to the buyers in Georgetown, if you feel up to it," Dad said, looking at his diamond watch to check the time.

"Yeah, no problem, Dad. How much do you think they'll be willing to pay for jewels like this?"

"I think you can get about fifteen thousand," Suitcase Murphy replied.

"Naw, man, I think she'll get a little more than that," Kid Twist said as he looked at me.

Dad said he would try to get thirty thousand, plain and simple. When it comes to the game, my dad is a very confident man and has been that way as far back as I can remember.

Dad and his partners briefly discussed another scam they were trying to pull off. They were talking about running a graveyard scam and needed a dead body to pull it off. They decided to purchase a *Washington Post* newspaper and look through the metro section for people who had funeral services that week. Dad wrote down a few places where he could show up and get the dead body he needed to make the scam payoff.

Twenty-five minutes later, we pulled up in front of the store where Dad planned to sell the jewelry. I stayed in the limousine while he made his moves. To pass the time, I put in a movie that was lying on the seat next to Kid Twist. It was a movie I had heard of before titled *Temporary Dreams.*

I sat in the long stretch limousine with my father's partners for little more than an hour before Dad returned. I had some anxiety over the situation because I didn't know whether Dad would make it out of the store or if he would get locked up or what. Sometimes things can get hectic or simply out of hand. Grifting wasn't easy, especially if you're a player, too. Not only was Dad a con artist, but he was a player, as well.

Dad pulled out a brown paper bag from his waistline and handed it to me. "Look in the bag, baby. You did well."

It was exciting to see just how much money he got for the jewels. When I looked into the paper bag, I saw a large stack of one-hundred-dollar bills. The sight of so much money made my pussy soaking wet. Since I was with my dad and his friends, I had to hold my composure, but if I had been with some fine-ass bitches, it would have been on like popcorn.

I'm like any other woman; money makes me cum. The first thing every woman thinks about is security and then money. Those two things are at the top of the list. Many times

I've had to play other people's games to get what I wanted. When most women are in relationships, they let their mate think he or she is running the relationship, but as long as you get your bills paid, or whatever your mate is providing, let them think what they want. As soon as they can't provide, blow them off like a bad habit.

I counted the stacks of money, which totaled forty thousand dollars even.

"Dad, how did you get forty grand?" I asked. "This is what the price was in the store."

"Baby girl, it's all in who you know," Dad responded, while rubbing my shoulder.

The chauffeur drove us to Dad's house. Once we got there, we saw about ten police cars, three detective cars, and the chief of police. They had my dad's house surrounded. We watched them bring the "key to the city" and knock his door straight in. We couldn't believe what we were witnessing.

Dad told the chauffeur to take us to a nearby Holiday Inn Hotel, where I booked a room for him for seven days. After he was checked in, we tried to figure out what were the police doing at Dad's house and why they knocked his door down.

"Daddy, why do you think the police were at your house?" I asked my father as he paced the hotel room floor.

"I'm really not sure, babe. I've been on the road with my

grifter for the last month. So, I can't say why."

"Do you think it may be because of the credit card scam we pulled when you dropped your ID?"

Suitcase Murphy sniffed six lines of cocaine. "This coke is good than a motherfucker, man."

"You're gonna snort it all up if you keep doing lines like that! Give me some of that shit, man," Kid Twist screamed out to Suitcase Murphy.

My father paced the floor for hours. During that time, we couldn't get a word out of him. He smoked cigarette after cigarette while walking from one side of the hotel room to the other.

"Dad I hate to see you like this. It's bothering me so much. What do we need to do?" I finally asked, as my father sat on the bed looking in the mirror at himself and not saying a word.

It was total silence among the four of us, and I didn't have a clue of what was going on. Normally, Dad would tell me everything, but in this case, he either didn't know what was going on or didn't feel comfortable with me knowing what was going on.

At that point, I just pulled out the brown bag full of money and handed my dad ten thousand dollars. Then I told him if he needed money for a lawyer, I would put money to the side. I also told him that I would be going back to San Francisco in a couple days, but if he needed me to take care of anything, just to let me know.

"Okay, that's cool," he said softly. "I'll keep you posted on everything."

I stood up from the chair I had been sitting in and headed out the hotel room door.

A few days later, I purchased an airline ticket back to San Francisco. I kept in touch with my dad on a regular basis just to make sure he was okay. When I arrived back in San Francisco, it was late. So, I met up with the girls at a club called Lick Dat Split, a strip club for female lesbians only. It was a real chill spot where some of the finest doms and fems stripped for cash.

One well-known dom dancer came over to the table where we sat, kissed me on my left cheek, and said, "I want to spoil you rotten."

I looked over at CoCo, who laughed and said, "That bitch better stop playing before she gets a serious beat down in this motherfucker!"

Mean Jean just sat there with a numb look on her face, one where I couldn't tell whether her thoughts were somewhere else or if she was just in a fucked-up mood. To be honest, I felt like those two had some dealings while I was gone or when I was out taking care of business. I could be wrong, but the better side of me told me something wasn't right.

The girls at the club looked good, and the female patrons were giving up cash to the dancers like bitches in a millionaire girls' club. CoCo and I had a few drinks, while Mean Jean drank water the whole night. That was good being that she was fresh out of rehab.

About three hours passed, and it was time for us to leave. As we drove to CoCo's place, I decided to give them the gifts I brought back from DC. I pulled out a diamond ring and matching watch for CoCo and a white gold necklace with a diamond cross for Mean Jean.

"Oh baby, you didn't have to do this for me. How could you afford this?" CoCo yelled out as I leaned over and kissed her sweet-tasting lips.

"I will never take this necklace off ever. This will go with me wherever I go," Mean Jean said, then kissed the back of my hand.

"So are you gonna ever wash your neck?" I asked, while Mean Jean continued to look at the gold necklace.

A good con artist always keeps people confused by doing something new and different at all times. Even if it's your partner, keep them wondering.

Chapter 16
THE WOMAN IN THE MIRROR

I came to San Francisco for a vacation and ended up in a relationship. I had my boss to hold my job down until I returned to Washington, DC. It's always about having people on your team, especially people on your job and mainly your boss. Even though I knew it was going to hurt CoCo, I felt it would be best for me to be back in DC.

I called my boss, telling her that I was coming back and had a big move for a large amount of cash. She was happy with the news since she was in desperate need of the money because she was behind in her rent and some other bills.

After getting off the phone with my boss, I thought about my plans and reasons for leaving CoCo without breaking a rule. What I mean by that is, never totally close the door on someone because you might need them again someday. However, if that person has too much fuckin' luggage in their life to the point where they are fuckin' crazy or it's no growth one way or another, close the curtain on them, and the sooner the better. That wasn't the case with CoCo Sweets, though. She was definitely someone who I wanted to keep in my life. I knew the rewards of having her, but I needed to return to Washington, DC where I could continue to make moves and stay in close contact with my dad.

When I got back to CoCo's place, she and Mean Jean were in the living room sitting on the couch talking. While standing in the doorway, I noticed Mean Jean had her right arm around CoCo. I wasn't mad, but it was just the excuse I needed to leave.

"I knew you bitches were cheating on me! Fuck both of you stinkin'-ass bitches," I said, while grabbing my luggage and setting it by the front door.

Mean Jean and CoCo pleaded with me, trying to convince me that they didn't have anything going on and that it was not what I was thinking.

"Sweetheart, I love you and no one else. I will never cheat on you," CoCo Sweet said as she tightly held on to my body.

"You are wrong, Envy. We would never do anything to hurt you," Mean Jean said.

I winked my eye at Mean Jean, but continued to play the role on CoCo like I was mad just so I could roll out. I called a cab, and fifteen minutes later, I was at the train station purchasing my ticket for the very long ride to DC.

When I got to the train station, I spoke with the person in customer service. The young woman directed me to the ticket counter, where I paid for my one-way ticket. Just so happened, the ticket agent got me into a sleeper train for my long journey back. At the same time, I pushed some game and got the bitch's name and number. I knew I would call her soon, because I needed her buddy passes to travel to the four corners of the world.

"Okay, ma'am, enjoy your travel back to DC. Remember, my name is Jackie."

"Oh, trust me, Jackie, I will be calling you. You're a beautiful woman that I would love to have as a special friend," I said and then ran for the track my train was leaving from.

Being she got me on a train that would be leaving within minutes of me buying my ticket, I felt special to her already.

I loaded my things onto the train and found my sleeper car. Right before I fell asleep, I heard other people talking in their sleepers. Each sleeper car had about eight different beds, some for a single person and some for an entire family. There were four top beds and four lower beds on each side of the sleeper cars. Each one had a curtain for privacy. I heard a woman talking on her cell phone and another man talking business. After that, I remembered nothing; I fell asleep.

A few hours later, I heard an Amtrak worker screaming at the top of his lungs as he walked down the aisle. "Tickets! Have your tickets out, please, so I can collect them. Thank you very much, ma'am," the worker said to an old lady.

Hours passed as I looked out my window. Getting a little hungry, I pulled back my curtain to go on a search for something to eat, and there stood the guy from the sleeping bed across from me. He was actually the one who I heard talking to someone about a business deal on his cell phone.

"Hello, how are you? My name is Dontaye," he said, extending his hand out for me to shake.

"Hi, my name is Envy. Nice to meet you," I replied.

"I'm about to go up to the dining car to grab something to eat. Would you like to join me?" Dontaye asked.

I clearly saw that he was an easy mark, so I decided to take him up on his offer. A free meal and the chance to take an application out on a new client? Sure. Why not?

"That will be fine," I said as I walked in front of him to the dining car.

We both grabbed chicken salad sandwiches and Sprites.

We sat at a table and ate while talking. I found out he was from Washington, DC, just as I was, and that he owned an entertainment company. *That's great,* I thought to myself, while Dontaye continued trying his best to make an impression on me.

Since he said his business was growing extremely fast and making money out the ying-yang, I started scheming on how I could steal his business right from under his nose if I ever saw him again.

We decided to exchange numbers. Then I went back to my sleeper and laid back down for several more hours before we rolled into Union Station. As passengers got off the train, I saw Dontaye once more before we went our separate ways.

I walked up to him, extended my hand, and said, "It was nice meeting you. Maybe we will see each other again someday."

"Yes, it would be a real pleasure if we do. I want to make a promise to you now before we depart."

"And what's that?" I asked as he shook my hand.

"I will spoil you with all that I can give you if we should ever become special friends," he said with a sincere look of appreciation in his eyes.

Although he didn't know I was a lesbian, I would play the game to get that money out of his ass. I don't chase mates. I chase their money like every woman should do…con women, that is. I look in the mirror at least three times a day and see myself as a commodity. I know my self-worth. Without knowing it, I would be setting myself up to be used and abused. Hell, I know what I want out of someone before they figure out what they only want from me. That's why it's important for you to look at what your game is and what you're selling, then figure out how to use it to get to the next level in your life. I know what my game is and how to utilize it to get to my next level. In my eyes, I got to cheat to eat. That's how it is in America.

Now, go look at yourself in a mirror and tell yourself what the fuck you want!

Chapter 17
SPLIT THAT CASH

About a year and a half later, my girlfriend and I were out for some drinks at XII Restaurant and Lounge on 12th & H Street Northeast. We were chilling, when suddenly I saw the face that I had been waiting to see for a long time.

"Hey, beautiful. How are you tonight?" the well-dressed man said.

"I'm fine. How about yourself?" I asked, looking the man straight in the eye.

"I'm here looking for sexy women like yourself to model for my entertainment company."

He went on to tell me about his company, and I remembered the same story on the train. He didn't remember me, but I sure did remember him. I even remembered the promise he made to me just before we went our separated ways. It was best that I let him start all over.

"We are steady talking and I don't know your name," I said.

I remembered his name from us meeting on the train, but I played the game like we were just meeting for the first time.

"Oh damn, my fault, baby. My name is Dontaye. What's yours?"

"I'm Envy, and I'm here with my cousin, Juicy. She just broke up with her man, so we're out celebrating," I told him.

I lied to him about Juicy breaking up with her boyfriend. Juicy was actually a lesbian, like myself. I just created a celebratory situation to see if he was a cheapskate or not. When running game, you must play people against their own egos. I knew if I did that to him he'd go out his way to prove to me that he had money.

"What? You some broke-ass dude or something?" I asked him.

"No, not at all, sweetheart. I can show you better than I can tell you. Here, take my card." He handed me his business card. "Get at me."

He then walked over to this sexy-ass woman that caused my mouth to water. I felt like a vampire geeking for some blood when I saw that sexy bitch. She had a serious-ass look in her deadly looking eyes, but that look got my pussy hotter than ever.

Even though I had framed Dontaye, he was a hustler in his own right. He was not on my level and not ready for what he was about to experience with me. I made it my business to dance with him a few times before he left the club because I wanted to get next to him. I needed to look him in his eyes and feel his spirit.

About a week later, I received a call from Dontaye. He wanted to meet for lunch. I told him that I couldn't have lunch with him that day, but I did tell him that he could stop by my office. He dropped by to see me at the hospital with flowers in one hand and an envelope full of large cash bills in the other. I couldn't believe it. He was a Class A mark, and it was so funny.

This is going to be like taking candy from a baby, I thought.

"Hey, babe. I thought I'd stop by and bring you something special," Dontaye said as he hugged me and presented the special gifts.

"All this is for me? Wow! I never had anyone come to my job and bring me nice things. Thank you so much, Dontaye," I said, giving him a big hug.

Touching is so underestimated. I was always taught to rub

143

someone's shoulder or arm or hold their hand because it gives them a since of security and genuineness. Great technique to use when you need to keep your mark fooled with confidence.

"So, how's your day going today?" I asked as Dontaye took a seat in a chair in front of my desk.

"Everything is fine. I just had to do some running around and take care of some business for my massage parlor," he replied.

I put the flowers in a vase of water and sat it on my desk. Dontaye went on to talk about his plans with his entertainment company. He told me that the girls who worked for him were making a lot more money than he expected, and he was looking to start investing money in the expansion of his company as far as representing and managing models. I kept the ball in his lap by letting him continue to share his business with me. Whenever he stopped talking, I thought of a question to ask to start him back talking about himself or his company.

"So what do you want with me, Dontaye? I'm not a model. I just have a pretty face with a phat ass and good-looking breasts," I told him.

"With you, Envy, it's different. I like what I see, and I think you and I could be real good friends."

I wanted to tell Dontaye that I was a lesbian and only interested in women, but he had two things that I was after: his money and his business. I had to do whatever it took to get in position to play him for his cash, even if I had to fuck him.

Dontaye and I ended up spending a lot of time together. I fucked him several times and it cost him some major cash, but I kept my focus. I had his money on my mind and my mind on his money.

A lot of lesbians would say it's not cool to fuck a man, but at the same token, they will drop their underwear and put their pussies up in the air for a nigga just like any other bitch. I kept in mind my reasons for fucking him and fucking with him. Unlike other women that would fall in love with men because they get caught up on the dick or be lonely for a man's company, I knew what my plan was as I moved in closer on him. Dontaye was a smart-ass dude; I had to admit that. He got a gang of lesbians to work for him and pay him with no sticky fingers in his pot. He was one bad motherfucker. I wondered what kind of game he fed them bitches.

Eventually, Dontaye took me with him to the massage parlor. That's when I met all of the girls and even got the chance to meet his mother, Rabbit. A few of the girls winked at me and talked to me about getting massages from them. There were about four of them who I wanted to have sex with, but before I did that, I had to figure out his daily routine. At the time, I didn't want to show I had any interest in any of them, so I did what any other bitch would do. I acted the part he wanted me to be and played the role I needed to play.

Chapter 18
TO LUST FOR A BEAUTIFUL WOMAN

Sitting in the massage parlor one night, I noticed all the women clients in the underground business. It was just as Dontaye said; the girls made so much money that it was unbelievable. Dontaye took a nap while we chilled at the parlor, so I took over for him watching the monitors and answering the telephones. I got the chance to look after the girls while they handled their business. One customer called and set up an appointment with Nikita Sunshine, and the things I saw when that lady got in the room were breathtaking. I was hornier than a female dog in heat.

Nikita Sunshine started out in the bathtub with the young woman. Nikita sucked on the woman's breasts. Then the woman positioned herself on the side of the tub and opened her pretty pink pussy lips so Nikita could lick her fat clit.

"Oh shit, baby. Your head is the bomb. Suck this pussy, sweetie," the young woman moaned.

Nikita Sunshine grabbed a long dildo and fucked the young woman until the lady busted a nut. I got turned on by the minute, my pussy bubbling with cum that ran down both my legs. I wanted her mouth on my pussy so bad that I sat at the desk and finger-fucked my pussy while rubbing my clit in a circular motion. I came and licked my damn fingers. My pussy tasted so good that I had to taste my damn self.

I was glad to have the chance to watch over the massage parlor. I looked forward to making myself right at home with Dontaye's business. As a matter of fact, I looked forward to owning the motherfucker.

A couple hours later, Dontaye woke up to the girls handing him a cool three thousand dollars. He came off real good being that he woke up to someone handing him a large stack of money like that.

After Dontaye counted his cash, he took the girls to Georgetown to grab something to eat. Tony and Joe's Restaurant is where we decided to sit and break bread. Everyone wanted lobster, so Dontaye ordered the lobster special for us. We sat talking and eating until everyone was about to bust wide open. After the meal, we had a few drinks and then headed out for a stroll down 14th and K Streets Northwest where all of the female prostitutes walked the block trying to catch a date and make that money.

During our outing, the girls and I had the opportunity to get a feel for each other. I felt comfortable with all of them, but I had to figure out how to win them over with confidence while corrupting them at the same time.

Dontaye walked to the corner to talk with two pimps named Sonny Redz and Johnny Black. As I stood there with the girls, we started talking about our goals in life and what we wanted to accomplish on earth before we die. Ghetto Storm said she wanted to become a millionaire and buy real estate for a living. Fantasy, Fame, and Nia Luv all wanted to be professional actresses and well-known celebrities. The femmes in the group, Sweet Money Reds, Nikita Sunshine, Kat, and Princess, all said they want to go to Las Vegas and open their own escort service. Wet Wet and Doneesha were the only two not sure what they wanted to do.

I had to convince the girls that they could make big things happen if they wanted. I shared with them how I made films and had many investors to finance my projects. I told them so many lies that they all looked hypnotized by the dreams and promises I made them believe.

"I can get y'all paid jobs to model for urban book covers, act in movies and lesbian porn films, and many other projects," I said, while the girls looked at me with excitement.

I told them that I was going to help Dontaye get to the next level with his entertainment company and have someone to write a movie script about his lesbian escort service.

"I believe he will get paid handsomely for this story. I don't think there's anything like it in Hollywood," I added as Dontaye started walking back down the street towards us.

I told the girls that they had to keep this a secret and not to tell him because I wanted it to be a surprise to him.

"Man, those pimps just told me that word is out about the parlor. Seems like a lot of pimps are jealous. They told me that I needed to be careful about who I deal with," he said after walking up to us.

From the look on Dontaye's face, he really didn't know how to take what the pimps had just told him. I could see he was a little intimidated, as well. Dad taught me how to read people. And from closely watching Dontaye, his moves showed insecurity. Therefore, I knew it was time to put my plan in effect.

Chapter 19

FEED THEM ALL FANTASIES

I finally got the chance to meet Dontaye's father, Creamy. I'd already met Rabbit, and from the looks of it, she seemed to be a crazy bitch that would eventually be my biggest problem. My father taught me how to play past certain people and situations, so I wasn't going to worry about her too much, not at that point anyway.

One day as I sat at the desk in the massage parlor, Rabbit walked in the door.

"Hello, and who in the hell told you that you can sit behind my son's desk?" Rabbit yelled as she approached the desk.

"Dontaye is taking care of some of our business. So, with me being his girlfriend, I will keep this place in order until he comes back," I replied calmly, while Rabbit stood close to the desk.

"Bitch, let me tell you one fuckin' thing. I don't know where you came from, but my son doesn't need you to help him with shit. You hear me, bitch?"

Dontaye told me how crazy his mother could get, and I wasn't there to do any fighting. So, I played past her and kept my focus.

"Rabbit, all I'm doing is what he asked me to do. If it were you that asked me to do something, I would totally take care of things just as you ask me to do," I told her.

"Well, Envy, or whatever your damn name is, I got my son's back, and I will beat you to death in this motherfucker if you think you can walk in here and cause problems. You hear me?" Rabbit screamed.

"Yes, Rabbit, I hear you. That's no problem," I responded.

Five minutes later, Dontaye walked into the massage parlor.

"Hey, Momma. What's wrong and why are you looking like that?" Dontaye asked Rabbit as he walked up to her.

"Ain't shit wrong! You better watch who you trust in this motherfucker. These stinking bitches these days ain't shit, ole funky motherfuckers!"

"Momma, just calm down. Everything is cool. Envy is my lady, and I trust her," Dontaye explained to his mother.

"Dontaye, I told Rabbit that I am only here to help you. I have no problem with her at all. I understand she wants things to be done correctly here."

"You right, bitch, and he needs to know that he don't need to be trusting no bitch at all! Dontaye, you better be careful. Something ain't right with that bitch," Rabbit said, then walked out of the massage parlor.

From that day forward, Dontaye tried to keep things cool between Rabbit and me. The girls told me that Rabbit would become jealous when someone gets close to Dontaye and for me to just play my cards right. I really didn't care about Rabbit or the way she felt about me being with Dontaye. Fuck her and the boat she rode in on. I had money to be made and wherever money is, that's where my pretty brown ass would be.

I fed the girls' fantasies about the dreams they told me about insofar as the life they wanted to live after leaving the massage parlor. I had some friends of mine to come to the massage parlor and shoot a thirty-second commercial. Of course, it was a phony shoot.

In order for me to stand out and look like the person that could take them to the promise land, I had to make them feel

153

important and show them that I could help change their lives, but only if they chose to follow me. I had to win the bitches' confidence, and it seemed like I was halfway there. I just needed to keep Rabbit out of my business and make sure those bitches didn't run their mouths to Dontaye or Rabbit. Then I could really get somewhere.

I told the girls that I would send the pictures to magazines and publishing companies. I fed them lies so they would sell Dontaye out, and I could make my move to take over the business.

I went up to Howard University College and put a film crew together. I invited the girls and Dontaye to the set as we shot a short film. I sat in a director's chair with the word DIRECTOR on the back and had a nineteen-inch monitor sitting in front as the cameramen were filming. I had all my actors and actresses in place as I shot the scenes.

"Quiet on set! Tape rolling and action!" I screamed.

We went on to shoot eight scenes in one location. It really had the girls excited about acting, and they were more than ready to sellout Dontaye in exchange for fame. It's my job to misdirect people and get paid well for doing it. Dad always said anything worth doing is worth doing well.

A few weeks later, I got the girls a photo shoot and promised I would send all of their pictures to different
154

magazine companies and publishing companies in hopes that they would be chosen for a magazine cover or book cover. It's all about what you sell to a mark, if you know what I mean.

Now, just to remind you, this shit was all fake: the photo shoot and the commercial. All the shit I told those hos was just to get them bitches to sell Dontaye out so I could move in and take the business. When you're on stage, as I call it, you have to make things look like what people want in their lives. You have to convince them to the point where they will trust you with the one life they were given. Always look the part when you're working your con game on the people you're conning.

Chapter 20

EVERY TOUGH BITCH WILL HAVE HER DAY

Many months passed, and things fell in place just the way I planned. One day while in the massage parlor with Dontaye, I decided to ask him if he would ever think about getting married. He gave me a strange look before telling me that he'd really have to know a woman really loves him before he just jumped out there like that.

A woman rang the doorbell and Dontaye buzzed her in.

"Hey, Sugar Momma. How are you, babes?" Dontaye said, hugging the woman.

"I'm fine. I thought about you, and since I was in the neighborhood, I figured I would stop by to see how you've been," the sexy brown-skinned woman said.

I gazed in her direction and our eyes met. There was an immediate attraction. I could tell she was interested in me, just as I was pretty much interested in her. At that point, it would only be a matter of time before we had moments together.

"Hi, how are you? My name is Envy," I said, shaking the woman's hand.

"Hey. They call me Sugar Momma," she quietly said.

Dontaye and Sugar Momma went into a back room. From the looks of it, they had some catching up to do since they hadn't seen each other in a while. About an hour later, Dontaye and Sugar Momma came out of the back room. As they were exiting the room, Rabbit was walking into the massage parlor, and as usual, Rabbit had something negative to say.

"You getting real comfortable with bringing these bitches in here, I see," Rabbit yelled to Dontaye as he walked with Sugar Momma to the front door.

"Bitch, you better watch who you call a bitch before you get your old ass fucked up!" Sugar Momma screamed back at Rabbit.

Rabbit and Sugar Momma walked up to each other, yelling and cursing in each other's face.

"Bitch, I never liked your funny-shaped ass. You walk around with all that tough jailhouse shit, but, bitch, you in the street now. It ain't hard to reach out and touch yo' motherfuckin' ass. So remember that!" Sugar Momma threatened.

"Yeah, and you remember this. It ain't hard to reach your ass either, bitch. I ain't tripping off your sucka ass. Who the fuck do you think you are?" Rabbit yelled as she pointed her index finger at Sugar Momma.

"Okay, bitch, I'll see you again, because I ain't going nowhere," Sugar Momma said before walking out the door.

"And I ain't going nowhere either!" Rabbit yelled.

Knowing that Rabbit and Sugar Momma really didn't like each other was to my benefit. All I needed to do was work a little magic to see whom I could make disappear. After the commotion between Rabbit and Sugar Momma died down, Dontaye sat in a chair next to me at the desk and told me that he thought something bad was going to happen between his mother and Sugar Momma.

"Sugar Momma and my mother are two dangerous females, and I don't like to be in the middle of this. I love my mother and I'll kill for her, but she can't keep treating people the way she does."

"Well, Dontaye, I think you need to keep Rabbit away

159

from here for a while before someone gets hurt," I told him, as he sat in the chair with his hands up to his face.

"Yeah, I know, but my mother is disrespectful and won't listen. She'll come anyway."

And Dontaye's mother, Rabbit, did just what he said she would do. She came to the massage parlor every day just to see if Sugar Momma had been there.

Now, on the other hand, Sugar Momma stayed away from the massage parlor, but she would call. I had the chance to talk with her on several occasions and informed her that Rabbit had been carrying a gun, so she may need to watch herself.

"So that's how that bitch wants to carry it? Okay, well, it's on, and I want you to keep your mouth shut about this. I mean don't tell anyone, including Dontaye," Sugar Momma said.

"I don't have anything to do with what's going on between you and that woman,' I replied.

Sugar Momma went on to tell me why she didn't like Rabbit and why she wanted to kill her a long time ago. This was just what I needed—a war between two bitches who needed to be out of the picture anyway.

Now you can see how people can remove themselves out of your way by their own doing. Do you understand what I'm saying? For example, you work on a job with someone who keeps a lot of shit started, and the two of you don't get along. At some point, that person ends up fucking with the wrong person, and either both parties get fired or the person that kept the shit started gets terminated. In most cases, those types of people get themselves removed from out of the picture. I learned to use that weakness to the best of my abilities.

Having Sugar Momma's personal number, I stayed in her ear as I set up the ultimate plan to get both of those bitches out my way as I moved in on Dontaye's business and took it right from under his nose.

Remember, life is what you make it. Many people in life settle on being stagnant at one level, while others continue to move up the ladder. I never knew what it took for someone else to get to the next level, so I found any weakness and manipulated to the best of my ability.

Chapter 21
FAKE IT TILL YOU MAKE IT

Sugar Momma called the massage parlor one night while Dontaye was out promoting Big D Entertainment. I think he was really looking for more girls for his sex chat line, but Sugar Momma told me that she wanted to be with me and asked that I leave the massage parlor. Sugar Momma and I had been fucking for several weeks and were with each other almost every day.

Regardless of how much I was around Dontaye, I found a way to get away and meet up with Sugar Momma. That woman had some good pussy. I ate her pussy for hours and let her cum in my mouth until she couldn't cum anymore. Sugar Momma liked to fuck me in the ass while I screamed out in pain. There's nothing like feeling pain and getting pain from someone you're in love with. I enjoyed the feeling of pain as I let Sugar Momma fuck me up the ass. I was fucked by the woman of my dreams. She was one hardcore, gangster-fucking bitch.

I got the chance to sneak away from the massage parlor to meet Sugar Momma. We decided to go to the Comfort Inn Hotel on New York Avenue. We took off our clothes the moment we crossed the threshold. The pussy-sucking, dildo-fucking, sweaty, ass-up-in-the-air escapade began. We fucked for hours, and it was all about sucking breasts, pussies, and assholes.

"I love sex. I am so fucking serious," Sugar Momma said as I licked up her ass from the back.

I put on a strap-on dildo and started fucking Sugar Momma from the back until she went fucking wild and damn near lost her mind. Every moment we were together felt like our first time.

When I got back to the massage parlor, my pussy and ass were hurting, but I enjoyed every bit of the pain. Dontaye started getting suspicious about me and began to think I was cheating on him with a man, so he called himself trying to set me up to catch me. I helped him by sending different people at him with ideas to catch me cheating.

I paid several men to be in an area or place where I knew

Dontaye would be. I told these men to strike up a conversation with him about a cheating woman and how to catch them. Dontaye had a few friends who worked at Howard University Hospital. One day, he told me that he was going up to Howard Hospital to see a friend that was in the hospital. I used that opportunity to trick him into telling me the room number so I could have someone posted up in the room waiting for him. I called my close comrade, James General, to assist me with getting Dontaye's money. I told him to act like he was spying on his girlfriend of five years.

James struck up a conversation with Dontaye about how good women cheat. Dontaye told James that he suspected me of fucking around on him, so James told him to put tape recorders in every room of my place and his place, as well. The misdirection he gave Dontaye was very important to play him and his ego. I was sure he would do some stupid shit to the extreme.

James sat in the room and talked to Dontaye for about twenty minutes, just enough time to plant the seeds and see what grew. At this point, I hadn't had sex with Dontaye for months, and being that Sugar Momma and I fucked like wild animals in heat, I didn't have the patience to fake like I was into men.

Later that evening, I invited Dontaye over to my place for

dinner. I told him that I went to the doctor, and they told me that I have tumors in my uterus and I won't be able to have sex for a while. He looked at me with a stunned look on his face. I thought I would just put that in his mind just before I set him up to snap. I still treated him with respect and did everything I could do to keep him feeling like he was my man. I even purchased him many gifts. I had to keep it looking good.

As we sat at my kitchen table eating salmon, brown rice, and kale greens, we watched as Channel 9 News reported a shooting that took place near the massage parlor. We saw some of the girls in the background crying as a female body lay motionless on the sidewalk. I looked at Dontaye and he looked at me.

"That's Rabbit lying on that sidewalk!" we both yelled.

Dontaye and I jumped up and ran out my front door. We got into his Mercedes Benz, and he drove as fast as he could over to the street where we saw his mother lying. By the time we got there, the police had the street sectioned off with the yellow tape. Dontaye ran up to the detective talking to paramedics as they were placing Rabbit into an ambulance.

"Excuse me, sir, but that's my mother who they just put in this ambulance. I would like to know if she's alive," Dontaye asked.

"Well, she's unconscious right now, and we are still investigating. Do you know of anyone who may have wanted to kill her?" the detective asked us.

Dontaye looked at me for a second.

"No, sir. I don't know of anyone who would try to kill my mother."

"Are you sure of that, because some witnesses said a female walked up and shot her a few times, while saying, 'What you got to say now, bitch? Show me how bad you are now.'"

The detective also described to us what they said the suspect looked like, including how tall she was, and the description fit the profile of Sugar Momma all day long. My plan was in effect and beginning to unfold. I could only laugh at that bitch on the inside. My first and last thought for her was, *Fuck that bitch.*

Chapter 22
ONE DOWN, TWO TO GO

When Dontaye and I finally got to Washington Hospital Center, the doctors had already started surgery on Rabbit. She was shot up pretty bad and had to go through surgery for about eight hours. Deep down inside, I knew Rabbit being shot was a result of her argument with Sugar Momma. Dontaye took the shooting hard because he knew Sugar Momma had something to do with the shooting, as well. I thought Dontaye was scared of Sugar Momma and really didn't know how to handle the situation.

The police were at the hospital still asking us questions, but we acted as if we didn't know anything. A few hours later, the detectives and police officials left.

Dontaye sat quietly most of the night. I couldn't get a

word out of him. At about seven o'clock the next morning, he came out of his daze.

"That bitch will pay for this. Nobody shoots my mother and thinks they will get away with it," Dontaye whispered softly.

We stayed at the hospital for three days before Rabbit gained consciousness. They moved her out of the intensive care unit when she became more stable and able to talk a little bit. Police officials returned to talk to her, but she cursed them out and put them out of her room.

"I don't know what happened, and you hot police motherfuckers can get the fuck out of my room!" Rabbit screamed.

"Momma, just calm down. They're here to find out what happened," Dontaye said, as Rabbit held her stomach where one of the bullets had entered her body.

"Those motherfuckers ain't here to help me. Would you hot-ass police get the fuck out of my room, please!" Rabbit screamed as loud as she could.

The police detectives and uniformed police all left out of her room, but not before one policeman yelled, "We'll be back!"

"Fuck you, and I'll be right here waiting, hot motherfucker!" Rabbit replied.

Two weeks later, on the day of Rabbit's release from the hospital, the police officials along with detectives came to her room to arrest her. She had an open warrant for assaulting two police officers. They had been looking for her for a while because assaulting the officers violated her parole. She was sent to DC Jail, where she waited for a trial date for her new charges. Eventually, she would be sent back to the federal penitentiary to serve out of the rest of her old sentence in addition to the new sentence she would receive for the assault.

It was back to business for me. I saw Sugar Momma a lot more. We went out of town from time to time to celebrate our newfound friendship and the fact that Rabbit was out of the picture. I also got the chance to get a lot closer to the girls at the massage parlor. I had them on the road with me making moves. I even educated them on how to be grifters. I was confident that they would become very skilled grifters at some point while under my umbrella...or should I say in my stable.

Dontaye did just what I wanted him to do. He planted voice-activated recorders all around my place so he could hear every conversation. He also put video recorders in his own place to see if I was bringing anyone over there, as well. For weeks, I had all types of conversations at my place to make it seem like it is what it is. I had to really get in his head to make him blow the motherfuckin' frame in the worst way.

I met men in clubs and had all kinds of conversations with them on the loud speaker. I talked about sucking dicks, how I liked to swallow cum, and how I liked to get my pussy ate. I said things to kill his spirit as much as possible. I imagined how his face looked every time he'd hear my moaning in the telephone or making all kinds of sounds as if someone was fucking my brains out. I even called a friend of mine on my job, put him on the loud speaker, and told him that I wanted him to meet up with two of my other male friends at my place so they could all run a train on me. I wasn't going to have sex with them, but I just wanted to get a reaction out of Dontaye.

Y'all know how men get when you tell them something like that. Men get so damn ecstatic when a woman tells them that they'll have a threesome with them.

Dontaye got the recorders and listened to them. That's when he started acting very strange, and it had gotten to the point where he wouldn't speak to anyone. The girls became paranoid of him at the massage parlor. It was like he had lost his mind. He wouldn't come to collect his money or check on the massage parlor or anything. I would collect money and give him most of it, but kept a few dollars for the girls and myself. It began to seem like he had so much on his mind that

172

he didn't know what to do.

After a few days, I went back to work at Greater Southeast Community Hospital, but during my lunch break, I met up with someone special at my place. We had only one thing on our minds and that was sex to the highest level. We tore off each other's clothing, and with every step to my bedroom, we performed some kind of sexual foreplay in a major fucking way. We kissed, we caressed, we sucked, we licked, and we fucked.

"Oh shit, that tongue is so damn good to me. Suck it, baby. Now put your finger in my asshole," I screamed as I got my pussy licked and finger-fucked in my ass. "Lick it and then spit on it. I'm your nasty-ass hoe, so treat me like a real hoe should be treated, baby. I want to lick your ass now, baby. Open it up wide for me," I yelled.

Cum ran down my legs as my special friend licked the warm, white, slimy liquid.

I enjoyed every bit of the sexual attention my body was getting, and I enjoyed giving attention just as much. My sex partner got on top of me and sucked my breasts, moving from one to the other. I enjoyed the feeling of wanting to feel something long, hard, and stiff in my soaking wet pussy.

"Oh my, oh my, oh my goodness." The licking and sucking on my hard nipples took me to extreme heights as my body trembled.

Have you ever had someone licking, sucking, touching and feeling on you so much that you just couldn't get enough of it? Well, that's just how it was for me. One thing people underestimate is the reaction that can be received from how much you touch someone, whether it's in the bed or just casually during conversation, and the feeling is much more intensified if the person is someone who is very close and special to you.

While enjoying the hot steamy sex with my favorite sex partner, I heard a loud voice scream out, "Bitch motherfucker, get your ass off my woman before I blow your damn brains out right now!"

My partner rose off of me, and I saw Dontaye pointing a gun at us. I didn't know how long he had been standing there watching us. I stood up with the covers from the bed wrapped around me.

"Dontaye, what are you doing here?" I asked.

"Bitch, what are *you* doing here? I figured you were cheating on me!" Dontaye shouted.

My partner looked at Dontaye, and Dontaye looked at my partner. We all got quiet as Dontaye walked over to my partner.

"Sugar Momma?" he said in a loud, confused voice,

grabbing the Afro bush wig from off her head. "You bitch! I got your ass now!"

Dontaye emptied the clip into Sugar Momma. Then he reloaded the gun, cocked the chamber, and shot himself in the head. I dialed 911 for help, went downstairs, sat on the porch, and waited for the police and ambulance to arrive to get them motherfuckers out my house. I played Dontaye the way a true player and con artist should have played him. I walked away with his money, his business, his girls, and his cars. I gained a lot just to make someone feel loved, huh?

All I can say is love ain't nothing but a hustle, so go get your hustle on!

CPSIA information can be obtained
at www.ICGtesting.com
Printed in the USA
BVOW06s0529210317
479025BV00002B/2/P